Ghost Town
Truck Stop

Barbara Paulding

Published by Happy Jack Publishing, LLC

Copyright © March 2014
by Barbara Paulding

First Printing April 2014

ISBN-10:0615999204

ISBN-13:978-0615999203

DEDICATION

This book is dedicated to my husband and best friend, Kirk Moody. He has supported me in this endeavor, as he has supported everything I have tried to do, completely, without reservation. He is truly "The Wind Beneath My Wings."

CONTENTS

ACKNOWLEDGMENTS

I want to say a special thank you to my editor and publisher, Beth Burgmeyer. Without her expertise and support, this book would never have been published. I cherish our relationship and am in awe of her abilities and professionalism.

I also want to thank my family for their encouragement and feedback. A special thank you goes out to my grandchildren: to Josh for keeping me going during my many edits and rewrites, and to Abby for doing the final reading of my book before it went to press.

Finally, I want to thank all of the men and women who do one of the hardest and most dangerous jobs in the world: the over the road, American truckers.

PROLOGUE

It is not a kind or gracious world that I inhabit. We, my fellow players and I, do not act out our parts against a backdrop of soft green lawns, pillared mansions, and the too sweet smell of magnolias. We do not spend our springs gathering fragrant sprigs of purple lilac, burying our noses in their wet fragrance. We do not walk barefoot in the late afternoon sun, grass still squishy underfoot, stirring the brown winter leaves in search of the timid crocus, the shy morels.

This is not the stuff our lives are made of. And if he sometimes buys me a rose, red and fragrant, from a street corner vendor, there is no waiting bud vase to protect its too transient beauty. I hold it close, mindful of the thorns, touch its soft sweetness with lips, nose. But it is not of our world. Not now. It is too soon dead, withered, lying brown on the dash, and I, I feel a desperate sadness at its passing. I have learned not to encourage such purchases, dear as the gesture is. Roses are not the stuff our lives are made of.

And if we sometimes catch a fleeting glimpse of such lives, such places, we stare in awe, amazement, feeling ourselves alien to their lives, their soft green worlds.

Sometimes, after we pass such a place, there is an aching, wanting cry born in us and we wish ourselves to be one with them. One with the young mother pushing a stroller down a tree shaded street. One with the young father returning home, predictably at

1

five, tie loosened, shirt sleeves rolled. One with the elderly gentleman gently loosening the black earth around his prized azaleas. One with their soft green world.

Such feelings do not last long. We have soon left their world and its quietude behind. The silent cry remains silent and silently sleeps once more.

Our world is neither soft nor green nor silent.

When I am tired, as I often am, I will not walk into my bedroom and slowly remove my clothes, will not wander through a sun drenched room, casually touching familiar objects. I will not fold back the quilt my mother made for me, a quilt exquisite in its simplicity. I will not lie between cool sheets. This is not the stuff our lives are made of.

When I am tired, as I often am, I stand up in the crowded cab and crawl over the doghouse to the bunk. I pull the curtains aside and lay down on the mattress, kicking clothes, tapes, maps, to one side. If I am not too exhausted I will sit up again and lean through the curtains to kiss him softly on the cheek, softly so as not to disturb his driving. I lie down then, pull the curtains tight, and try to sleep. The big diesel hums, drones, and I soon feel my eyelids grow heavy.

In a few hours he will stop and I will wake to the soft "psst, psst" of the air brakes. We will go in together, I still tangled in leaden sleep, he weary, muscles cramped, eyes red, another of the endless cigarettes he smokes dangling from his lips. He will cough as we walk across the big parking lot and I will feel my stomach tighten in anxiety. He smokes so much.

Sometimes it is summer when we walk across the parking lot and we squint our eyes as the sun bounces up at us off of the hot concrete. Sometimes the parking lot is not paved and the dust blows mercilessly into eyes and nostrils. Sometimes it is cold and the wind whips at us, ice is everywhere underfoot, and the trip from truck to truck stop door is a seemingly endless one. I do not like the cold.

We sit down to dinner then, he weary with too much driving, I yawning, feeling myself reluctant to leave sleep's peaceful depths. At such times I will excuse myself and go off to wash my face and brush my teeth. Sometimes the places I retire to are adequately clean and I feel somewhat refreshed and renewed. Sometimes the filth is such that I hesitate to reach out and touch the faucet to turn on the small stream of brownish water that I know awaits me. I do not like these places but I have learned not to cry about them.

When I return to the dining room, I look around at my fellow players, wondering about their lives, their longings.

Soon it will be time for us to leave. I will not be here again. When we sit down tomorrow it will be in another truck stop a thousand miles down the road.

We climb back in the truck. It is my turn to drive, to stay awake. He settles himself in the bunk, admonishing me to be careful.

I will drive until I too am weary, muscles cramped, eyes heavy, demanding sleep. I will pull over then and climb in the bunk. He will stir slightly, reaching for me in his sleep. He will hold me close and I too will soon sleep, lying content in his arms.

Sometimes my contentment will last for hours, last until dawn's timid light wakes us out of exhaustion's sleep.

Sometimes my contentment is too quickly gone, broken not by dawns' light, but by a knock on the door, a knock both questioning and demanding. I will hear her voice then, a young female voice, asking him if he would like some company. If the voice is street wise and Brooklyn tough I will roll over, disgruntled but undisturbed and find sleep again.

It is only when the voice is light, sweet, seemingly innocent, that I will wake fully and sit up shivering, pulling the blankets close. You see, I will imagine it is Jennifer who knocks on our door, she who is smiling sweetly up at my husband, she who is standing below us hands stuffed in the pockets of her short fur coat, blonde hair curling softly on her shoulders.

3

Sometimes I feel myself compelled to get up and go to the window, so strong is the feeling that it is she who is standing there below me. I pull myself from the warm certainty of our small bed, looking expectantly down at the figure standing in the moon's cold light. It is never she, just some sad young thing with small, dry tits and dirty knuckles.

Sleep does not come easily after such encounters with the past.

Ghost Town is with us still.

I see it as it was then, lovely beyond description, weathered shake shingles, wide plank sidewalks, hitching posts, fragrant pines, brilliant cardinals and saucy jays at the feeders and everywhere the snow.

Ghost Town and its ghosts. Jennifer. Katie. Rob. Old Jeremy. Preacher Man. Brad and Sandy. They are all here, trapped in time, trapped by the written word, trapped now, as they were trapped then, by the snow and the cold and the long tenacious tentacles of times past that seem to follow all of us everywhere.

Trapped. Trapped at the Ghost Town Truck Stop just off the interstate in the middle of nowhere in the middle of Montana.

MONDAY
January 13, 1985

CHAPTER ONE

Jeremy liked Ghost Town, liked it best like this. Pre-dawn. Sleeping monsters. He rode his bicycle up and down the rows, noiselessly, weaving in and out between the big semis, marveling at their size. His long overcoat flapped around his knees as he pushed the pedals up-down, up-down. January and still no snow. But he could feel it in the air, knew it would be here soon. Jeremy chuckled to himself. *Bet I won't be riding this bike tomorrow.*

Jeremy pulled his coat closer, glad for its warmth. Someone, sometime, had given him that coat. It had been almost new then, soft, warm, with a row of shiny brass buttons. It was old now, old and buttonless.

Old coat. Old man. Ageless old man. Comic borrowing children, now adults with children of their own, saw the same scraggly beard, engineer's hat, smile.

He lived alone, was never lonely. His one room cabin and small yard were filled with wonderful creations, his creations, all painted red, white, and blue.

One side of his cabin was covered with the names of all the presidents of the United States. Beside each name he had their hometowns and dates of birth. Each number, letter, had been painstakingly cut from old linoleum, all painted red, white, and blue.

People came sometimes, to talk, to take pictures of his sculptures, his president's wall.

People came, sometimes. The children always came. They stopped by his cabin to read his old comic books, to talk. Some of them, the ones with the quiet hearts, learned the old games from Jeremy: mumblety-peg, marbles, jacks, learned to whittle, to make whistles out of tender green willow sticks.

Marbles was Jeremy's favorite. The circle in the dust, round, complete. The fancy marbles with the candy cane stripes inside, the shooters, the homely little brown and white speckled ones. He loved them all. "Knuckle down," he would tell the kids. "Knuckle down, skinny bone tight."

Sometimes he showed them how the size of the circle could make the game all different, all mixed up. If he made the circle too little, it was too easy to shoot the marbles out. If he drew a huge circle, nobody, not even Old Jeremy, could shoot the marbles past the edge.

He would get excited then, eyes lit up. "See? See here?" he would say to the children. "Circle has to be right. Find the right size circle and it all works. See?"

The children. Children of other children. The circle, round, complete.

Jeremy had almost completed his circle when he saw a few truckers making their way to the famous Ghost Town restaurant for breakfast. Jeremy waved to them, smiled. They always waved back, looking surprised, startled. Jeremy smiled to himself. He had heard all of the stories, stories that claimed he was really a ghost, the ghost of Ghost Town. Katie knew, knew he was no ghost, told him he was a guardian, the Ghost Town guardian.

Jeremy chuckled. *Time for this old ghost to go home, get warm, get ready for the snow.* Time to complete the circle. Jeremy's circle. Down Canyon Road. Around Ghost Town. Up Blackjack Road to the path below the mountain, the path that led him back to his cabin. His cabin. His circle. Just the right size. Round. Complete.

CHAPTER TWO

Kathleen O'Connor was having her kind of morning. She woke up slowly, lit a fire in the fireplace, and was now back in bed working on her second cup of coffee.

She looked around her room. Stark whites. Soft blues. Cat Stevens was singing to the new day.

Katie felt at peace, was grateful for that peace, said a small prayer. "Thank you, God. For letting me heal. For this morning." Then she grinned. "And please don't let me turn into a self-satisfied little shit. Amen."

Katie smiled again.

How good it was to sit like this, doing nothing. How good it was to feel peaceful inside, to feel whole, safe, close to God.

The other, the pain, the rage, that terrible wanting to howl at the moon sadness, was a part of her past. Past. Gone.

Forever? she wondered, picking up a small hand mirror, studying her face.

"What do you see when you look in the mirror, Katie O'Connor?" Joe's question. Joe's voice. So long ago. Indian Joe. Her Joe.

"Me. I see me, Joe," she said to the quiet, empty room.

It was an early fall afternoon. The sun warmed leaves crackled underfoot and everywhere a faint, shimmering trace of smoke lingered in the air. Dreamers dreamed of brown skinned Indians, teepees, of grasslands and massive beasts.

Indian Summer.

Indian Joe, her Joe, sweaty, triumphant, surrounded by cheerleaders and pompom girls.

Twelve year old Katie leaned against the fence that ran behind the track field.

They were so stupid, those girls, stupid and giggly. Katie hated them, hated their skimpy little skirts, their brown legs, their flashing smiles.

> "Oh, Joe! You were so wonderful!"

> "Joe, you are coming to my party aren't you? Pleease."

> "Want a ride home, Joe? I've got my dad's new car."

"Oh, Joe!" Katie mumbled to herself, mocking them.

Sixteen year old Joe smiled at the girls and excused himself, looking around for Katie. He saw her over by the fence. She was wearing a pair of scruffy blue jeans, her long, curly hair was pulled back from her face. Katie.

He walked over to her. "How'd I do, coach?" he asked, kiddingly. Then he saw the tears in her eyes. "What's wrong, Katie?" he asked.

"Nothing. I just, I'm…" Misery and twelve year old honesty won out. "You have all those girls crazy about you and I'm just not anything like them. I'm plain and ugly and…"

Joe shook his head in disbelief. He held her at arm's length, looking her up and down, appraisingly. "Nope," he said. "Nope, you're not anything like them." Then he grinned. "Thank God."

He threw his arm across her shoulder in the old way, the easy way. "Those girls don't like me. They don't even know me. They just like my fast feet. Now as for being plain and ugly, well before you go to sleep tonight, you look in the mirror, really look, and then tomorrow morning when we go out to run I want you to tell me what you saw. Okay?"

"Okay," she said.

The next morning he asked her what she saw when she looked in the mirror. "Me," she said. "I saw me. I'm just not..." She stopped, not knowing the words. "Not fancy," she said, inadequately.

"Know what I see? When I look at you?" he asked.

"What?" she asked, sensing something new, something that made her cheeks feel hot.

Joe didn't look at her. He kept his eyes fixed, far away. "See a funny little face. Freckle dusted nose. Blue eyes. Springtime eyes. Long, curly, black hair. Black enough to be a Cheyenne but too damn curly." He looked at her then, grinned, grabbed her by the hair. "Course we could braid it, disguise it sorta. Then maybe, just maybe, we could pass you off as a member of the tribe." He shook his head, sadly. "Nope. Couldn't do that. No Cheyenne could possibly run as slow as you." He laughed.

"Joe!" she said, half laughing, half mad.

They started wrestling, fell down. Sun warmed leaves. Joe looked down at her. "You are beautiful, Katie. So beautiful." He brushed her lips softly with his.

Katie put her arms around his neck and pulled him close.

The kiss was longer this time. Heart pounding.

Joe scrambled up and reached down for her hands.

"I love you, Katie. Even though you're plain and ugly and an ornery little kid, I love you. But I'm not ever gonna kiss you again. Not until you're old enough. Understand?"

"When will I be old enough?" she asked.

"How the hell do I know? How come you keep asking all these questions? I guess you'll be old enough when your mom lets you go out on dates. C'mon now, race me down to the end of the road."

They ended up as they always did at Old Jeremy's cabin. If it was sunny and warm they stretched out on the bank in front of his cabin, letting the sun dry the sweat from their bodies. If the day was cold, they went inside, camping out by the fire, fighting over comics.

"Remember this one, Joe. I think it was the first one I was able to read on my own."

Joe glanced over at Katie. "Yeah, I remember, Tarzan, you were always trying to swing from the trees." He smiled at her, messed up her hair.

Old Jeremy loved them, had watched over them, taught them the old stories, games, and here they were almost grown, still letting him watch over them.

Old Jeremy. Joe and Katie. Every time they left Jeremy's cabin, they left together, hands clasped, Joe dancing on his toes, teasing, wanting to run and run… "Come on, Katie, race me down to the end of the road."

"Race me down to the end of the road. Race me…"

Joe started running when he was in sixth grade. The school held a fun race and Joe ran that race as he had run all his life, joyfully, freely, black hair flying in the wind.

By the time he was a freshman he was running with the varsity cross country team. He went to state that year, came in second. It was the only major race he ever lost.

Fast feet. The only major race, until he lost it all, lost himself, in a faraway jungle in Viet Nam.

When Katie turned eighteen, she felt she was on the cusp of life, sure that her dreams of a life with Joe were about to come true. But those dreams turned out to be as insubstantial as the mist that hung over the hills on summer mornings.

Joe, a senior in college, glory bound, America's best hope for gold in the upcoming Summer Olympics, told Katie he planned to enlist in the army.

Katie cried when he told her his plans.

"Why, Joe? Why?"

"Why? God, I just have to. I can't live with it anymore."

"Live with what, Joe? Live with what?"

"I don't know," he said slowly. "The guilt I guess. If I weren't fast I wouldn't be in college. I would never have had the money to go. So, by some quirk of fate here I am, safe, protected. All the others, the guys who couldn't afford college or just weren't right for college? They're being drafted, sent to Nam, fighting, dying. It's just not right."

"But you don't even believe in this war. You hate it. You've said so lots of times."

"I know, I do hate it. But the method of selection is wrong, all wrong. Selective Service? That's a good name for it. Selective as hell. Selects all the guys who want to be electricians instead of doctors and lawyers. I don't know, it just eats me up. It's something I had to do, to protest. People have made a big deal out of what I've done, why I've done it. Maybe something will change. Maybe they'll throw all the names in a hat and draw them out fairly."

Katie didn't care about the morality of it all, about the inequity of the draft, all she cared about was Joe, her Joe.

When he finished basic training she flew to Georgia to be with him.

"Are you old enough to go out on dates yet, Katie O'Connor?" he asked her when she got off the plane.

She shook her head yes.

Joe held her close. "I think we better get married, Katie."

So they got married, tried to live a lifetime in the two weeks before Joe shipped out.

At first there were letters, she saved each precious word, wrote to him every day, told him about the miracle that was happening, the baby that was growing inside of her, their baby. Then nothing. Katie continued to write everyday but there were no more letters from Joe. The only thing that came home from Vietnam was a box, just a box. There wasn't any Joe in that damn box.

Joe's belly was full of shrapnel. Katie's belly was full of baby. Joe's warm young body was blown to pieces. Katie's warm young body was blossoming, expanding.

Katie did not want to have anything to do with any part of blossoming, with anything, anybody.

The baby paid no attention to her wishes. It kept growing. One day it kicked her hard, up under her rib cage.

Katie gasped, grabbed her stomach. *Fast feet,* she thought, half laughing, finally able to cry.

CHAPTER THREE

It was Indian Summer when Little Joe was born, sliding out into the world, red face screwed up, fists flying. Katie touched his tiny fist, it opened, held her finger tight, held her heart.

Little Joe had his father's black hair and bronze skin. When Katie looked at him she saw Joe's solemn black eyes looking back at her, saw Joe's slow smile, gentleness.

Katie's life had meaning again. She returned to school, determined to finish her classes, to become a teacher. When she went to class she left Little Joe with her mom and dad. Sometimes she took him to Jeremy's, knowing he would watch over her son just as carefully as he had watched over another little black haired boy with solemn eyes. No nameless, faceless strangers would ever care for Little Joe.

Katie started teaching when Little Joe was five. He walked proudly beside her into the sunny little kindergarten classroom, sat quietly, taking it all in. When school was over for the day he slipped his hand in hers and they walked together to the car, took the short drive home.

Every night when Katie tucked him in, kissed him good night, she told herself that he was safe. Little Joe was safe.

He was safe and then he was dead. Dead. One day he was a healthy five year old with a crooked grin. Forty-eight hours later he was a still, lifeless corpse.

"Spinal Meningitis," the doctor said, in his very best funeral tone.

"So sorry...so sorry. Nothing we could do, do, do. You'll have to calm down, down, down. Other patients, patients, patients. Now, now, nowoow..."

It all hurt too much, everything blurred and hurting and faces and arms and Mom and Dad and they wanted to hold her, comfort her, and *no, oh no, not now, not me, just go away, comfort the comfortless*, she screamed inside her head, pulling away from them.

Katie left the hospital, the town, coat flying wild in the wind, face a white, set mask. "Fast feet," she screamed at the still, silent sky. "Fast feet. See Joe, see Katie run, see, see Little Joe. He's dead, Joe. Dead. Dead, damn you. Why'd you leave me here, leave me all alone, damn you, damn you to hell and back..."

Her parents drove through the small town looking for her, but Katie was gone. They contacted the police, went home to wait.

It was late that night when Old Jeremy found her. She was lying on the bank of the small stream that ran behind his cabin, arms clasped around her knees, hair matted with mud and leaves. A soft rain began to fall and she lay there trembling, whimpering, under her already wet coat.

Jeremy went to find her mom. He knocked shyly on the door, engineer's cap in his hand. "It's your little girl, ma'am," Jeremy said. "I, I found her. Up by the stream. I think it's some poor animal howling, hurt. It's your little girl, ma'am, Joey's girl. She won't come with me."

Her mother grabbed her coat.

CHAPTER FOUR

H owl at the moon sadness.

> No more tears, lady.
> Not now. Not today.

Katie looked at the clock, surprised to see that it was early afternoon.

> Get to work, Katie O'Connor.
> Move. Now. Ghost Town
> Truck Stop awaits the arrival
> of its clutsiest fuel attendant.
> That's you, lady. Move.

She got up slowly.

Katie walked into her office at Ghost Town a little after two.

"Paul Danvers wants to see you, Katie," her secretary said.

Katie smiled at the girl. "Okay, Lisa. Just let me get my coat off."

A few minutes later Paul, one of the security guards, was sitting across the desk from her.

"I'm a little concerned about this one truck, Katie. It's been parked in the same place for days. Hasn't been moved. I don't know if the driver just walked away and left the damn thing or if he's still around."

"You better check it out, Paul. See if there's anybody in there. If it's been abandoned just notify the company and they can send somebody out to pick it up. If the driver's in the truck, make sure that you tell him, or her, that we just wanted to make sure they were okay. I don't want drivers to get the feeling that they're being hassled by security. Okay?"

Paul nodded and picked up his jacket.

"Paul?"

"Yes, Katie?"

"Check back in with me after you find out a little more. I'll probably be out at the fuel pumps."

CHAPTER FIVE

The sleeper berth was warm, curtains zipped tightly down, heater pumping out dry, stale air. The bottles of Bud he had downed last night stood in an uneven row on the doghouse outside the bunk. Some of the bottles were empty, some half filled with piss.

Beer and piss. Piss and beer.

Ashes to ashes, dust to dust.

Beer to piss, piss to beer.

Abraham was still asleep when the knock came on the door.

He woke up, reached across the doghouse to unroll the window, knocking over a half filled bottle of piss. "Goddamn, son of a bitch," he muttered.

He rolled his window down and felt the biting wind hit his bearded face. The sweet smell of stale beer and the acid stench of urine seeped out of the window, down to the man standing at his door. Abraham stared down at the man, felt his pulse quicken. It was a security guard.

"Sorry to bother you," the guard said. "Just wanted to be sure you were alright, see if you needed anything."

Abraham forced a smile to his lips and exaggerated his good ole boy drawl. "Why thank you kindly, officer, thank you kindly. Just needin' a little sleep."

The security guard nodded. "Okay, just let us know if you need anything." He turned and walked away.

Abraham pulled himself back in the bunk, wiping the sweat off of his forehead. "Thought they had come for me," he mumbled.

Thought she had talked. Whore. No reason for me to be so scared. She liked it, liked it just fine, opened her legs fast enough. Scared, so scared when the knife came out.

Abraham rolled over and stared up at the ceiling of the bunk. Whore. She was the one to blame, all her fault. Looking at him in that bar Saturday night. Women were always looking at him, commenting on his coal black hair and striking blue eyes. This one was no different. Coming back with him to the truck stop. Climbed willingly in his truck, his bunk. Whore. She had been so scared when she saw the knife. A scared whore. He smiled, remembering. Saw her face suddenly pale. Pasty.

"What, what are you doing?"

The knife slid over her soft belly.

"God, don't hurt me, mister. Please, just let me go."

Abraham's lips curled up in a smile. His instrument that had lain soft and lifeless was now forged with strength, erect, hard as steel. Forged, like the hard, shiny blade he held in his hands.

He moved the blade again, talked to her, his voice soft. "Which one shall I put in you, whore?" He grabbed her by the hair, shook her, hard. "Look at me, whore. Tell me what you want."

The girl sobbed. "You, please just you. No knife. Don't hurt me, please don't hurt me. Just let me go home. I want to go home, I…"

He moved the knife again. Dropped it on the floor. Entered her, exploded instantly.

When he rolled off of her, the girl scrambled up and ran, ran barefoot, into the cold January night. Abraham called after her. His head rolled back, his eyes stared straight ahead. Words, long buried but not forgotten, rolled off his tongue.

"Then they shall bring the damsel
to the door of her father's house

19

and the men of the city shall stone
her with stones that she die:
because she hath wrought folly in
Israel to play the whore in her
father's house."

Abraham's voice strengthened, picking up the revival rhythm, the rhythm of his childhood. HIS rhythm.

HIS rhythm, revival rhythm, southern rhythm. That rhythm had been Abe's rhythm, that world, Abe's world, once, long ago.

Abraham Elijah Samuels was born and baptized some forty-three years ago in rural Georgia.

It was a small world.

Abe.

Mama.

The farm. Hot, dusty, sleepy summers.

HIM.

HIM.

HE came every summer, as predictable as the flies that buzzed around the fresh cow pods in the pasture. HE came with the summer heat, came when there had been no rain for days and days, came when dust clouds stirred with your every step as you walked down the silent country roads.

That's when HE would arrive.

HE was tall, bigger than life, with a shock of black hair that fell below his white preacher's collar.

HIS eyes were blue, icy, blue, piercing eyes. If hell had a color it would be that color, the color of HIS eyes.

HIS voice was unlike other voices. It cajoled, softly, seductively, made you want to be close to HIM. Thundered, made you want to run to your room and hide, not come out until the storm was over.

Thunder and Lightning.

HE was in their house. Little Abe watched him eat, fascinated. HE had eaten and eaten. Now there was a big bowl of fresh cobbler in front of HIM. HE swallowed that up too, leaned back in his chair, satisfied.

"That was a fine meal, sister," HE told Abe's Mama. "A fine meal from a fine woman."

Abe's Mama's face was flushed and her hair was curled softly around her little girl's face. Her eyes shined from HIS words of praise.

Later HE called Abe into the parlor. Brother Michael. Boots off. Black preacher's coat unbuttoned. HE put his hands on the little boy's shoulders, asked him questions, voice warm, kind. Eight year old Abe stuttered shyly. HE was patient. The little boy gained confidence. Glowed. HE loved him a little. Maybe?

HIS eyes changed. Ice. "You messing with the little girls yet?" HE asked.

"No, sir," Abe said, not knowing what was meant but knowing he shouldn't be doing it, whatever it was.

"You play with your little thing at night, boy?" HE asked, sternly jovial.

Abe shook his head no.

"You take your pants down, boy, let me check you out, see you behaving yourself."

Abe squirmed uneasily.

"You do what you're told, boy," HE said, eyes icy.

Abe slid his suspenders off his shoulders and dropped his britches.

HE leaned forward, looked at Abe's privates. "You touch yourself, boy? Like this?" HE asked, moving his hand over Abe's little thing.

"No, no, sir," Abe stuttered. "No."

"At night?" HE asked, softly, seductively. "After your fine mama's asleep?" Still moving HIS hand.

Abe felt all funny inside. He shook his head no again.

The hand became cruel, squeezed him. "You lyin' to me, boy.

Boys always play with themselves. God don't like you to do that, boy. You remember that."

Little Abe's eyes were full of unshed tears.

The hand became softer again, the voice soft. "God don't want you to do this to yourself. Remember that, son, remember God don't like little boys that play like this."

The hand was gone.

"You play with yourself it'll fall off, then you won't grow up to have a big fine instrument for the Lord, like me." HE laughed.

HE was breathing funny. HE pulled HIS thing out of HIS black preacher's pants and it was huge. It was like HIM, bigger than life. "See, boy, you follow the Lord, don't abuse yourself, you grow up big like this."

HE leaned back in the chair and closed HIS eyes, sighed deeply.

"Can I put my pants on now, sir?" Little Abe asked.

HE nodded, not opening his eyes.

Abe pulled up his britches and walked quietly out the door. He went out to the barn, climbed up in the hayloft, took out his little thing and looked at it.

> "You play with yourself, boy?" he heard the voice asking, over and over. "You play with yourself, boy?" Abe felt all funny, warm, touched himself the way HE had touched him.

Abraham tossed restlessly in his sleep, in his too warm bunk. His hand found his half erect prick, moved over it, gently, like HIS hand. Abraham heard HIS voice again. "You play with yourself, boy? Like this, boy? You play with yourself?"

"God damn right I do, Preacher Man," he mumbled. "God damn right I do."

CHAPTER SIX

Afternoon light.

Jennifer had chosen the small apartment because of it, had first seen it on a warm sunny day in June.

Afternoon light. Good light.

In the middle of the rooms' light was a long piece of plywood resting on two sawhorses, paint, canvas, and a young girl.

Jennifer.

Her slender young body was dressed in scruffy blues. Jeans, an old denim shirt, high top sneakers, laces loose, untied.

Jennifer. She was so beautiful that when people first saw her they would catch their breath, feel an aching want, feel that they wanted to somehow protect her, her beauty, her innocence.

She had been working on the painting for weeks and was still not satisfied with it. Katie's face was there on the canvas, looking up at her. Katie's deep blue eyes were alive with warmth and laughter. But the shadows of sadness that also lived inside of Katie continued to elude Jennifer's brush.

The day's light started to fade. Jennifer pushed her hair back and reluctantly put away her paints. She sat down in the one chair in her room and looked at the clock.

Almost time for work, she told herself. *I better get a shower and wash off this paint.*

Two hours later she was walking down the street toward Ghost Town, leaving the little town of Guardian, Montana behind. The scruffy denims and high top sneakers had been replaced. Jennifer walked down the street with a quick, light step, cosmopolitan fashionable in her black slacks, high heeled black boots and short fur coat. It wasn't a long walk. Her apartment was at one end of the long Main Street in Guardian. Once she crossed over the bridge on the interstate, went past the motel where the tired truckers sometimes stayed, she was almost there.

When Jennifer reached Ghost Town she entered a side door and headed to the gift shop for her evening shift.

Truckers came in, stared, tongue tied. Jennifer smiled sweetly at them, flirted, ran her tongue over her lips, teased, smiled again, a smile so practiced it seemed real.

Jennifer knew exactly what she was doing, exactly how she was affecting those lonely truckers, felt a familiar, small, mean satisfaction as she watched them stumble from the gift shop, arms loaded down with unplanned purchases.

Too bad, truckers. No Little Jennifer in your bunks tonight, she thought, feeling a little ashamed, feeling sick to her stomach.

CHAPTER SEVEN

Rob had been driving steadily since early morning and he was still a good two hours from Ghost Town.

Just before dark he stopped at a rest area and leaned back in his seat. His right knee felt stiff and painful. The back of his neck hurt like hell. He slowly climbed out of the big old Pete and moved around, loosening up his stiff body.

It was a cold, grey, Montana in January day.

What the hell am I doing in Montana in January? Rob wondered. *Forty some years old and here I am still driving around in a damn truck. Shit. Should have quit years ago, quit when Randy left…* He climbed back in the truck and headed down the road.

Rob should have been born a hundred years earlier, born in a time when a man could throw a leg over a horse, ride off, live. Cattle drives, dusty cow towns, and round ups. Squalling calves, the smell of coffee and beans, leather and sweat.

Should have been.

Wasn't.

When Robert Townsend turned twenty there were no more cattle drives, no more Chisholm Trails, no more new frontiers, no more leather and sweat.

His rodeo days were over, compliments of a rank, piebald mare he had drawn at the national finals a year earlier. Shattered knee. Shattered dreams.

One day, when he had nothing better to do, he wandered into a small trucking company in East Texas and asked for a job.

The man behind the desk looked skeptically at the tall, blonde haired young man with the cocky grin. "Ever drive a truck, sonny?" he asked.

"Yes, sir," Rob said. "Been driving for a year. Eighteen wheelers."

"Bullshit," the man said.

Rob turned to leave, shrugging his shoulders, a smile on his face.

Just before Rob reached the door, the man's voice stopped him. "Wait a minute, hotshot."

He threw a set of keys to Rob, walked out to the parking lot with him, gave him a two hundred dollar advance and told him to take a load to Albuquerque.

By the time he was a hundred miles down the road, Rob had almost figured the gears out. Twenty years later, when it was still wide open, he had owned a whole string of trucks, new trucks, the best, hired the best drivers.

The best trucks, the best drivers, Randy. He had it all then, loved it all.

Until the divorce.

Eight years now.

The divorce took place in an orderly fashion. Rob willingly gave her the house, the money in the joint checking account, and a percentage of the business. And it hurt like hell. He felt so damn guilty and scared and he had this terrible, sad, quiet sense of shame. To have failed, failed at what should have been the most important thing in his life, failed at marriage. Divorced. He felt like a god damn statistic, like, like a failure.

It hurt like hell.

But he still had the boy and he still had the trucks. And every

Friday, as soon as school was out, every vacation, all summer long, Randy rode the trucks with him, just as he had from the time he was a baby.

"Let him go with me, honey."

"Rob! He's just a baby. Still in diapers. What are you going to do when he cries? Wets?"

"I'll take care of him. It's just a one night run. He'll like it. Sleep while I'm driving. Come on, honey."

And the girl with the auburn hair smiled at him and hugged him and laughed and the boy went with him.

Randy learned to steer the damn things long before he could reach the pedals, learned to shift the gears, learned it all sitting on his dad's lap. And the crazy little kid loved it, loved it as the man loved it, as the man loved him.

So, as bad as it was, the divorce thing, as bad as it was, it was bearable.

That lasted for a year, lasted until the lady who used to be his wife, but wasn't anymore, went back to court and convinced the judge that her renegade, truck driving, ex-husband, was a bad influence on their sixteen year old son, Randolph.

Her lawyer made a strong case against Rob, using the last run the boy had made with him as final proof that Rob was an unfit parent.

A sleepy little Mississippi town. A scale.

Every time a trucker went past that scale late at night, the weigh master played a cruel little cat and mouse game with them. He would wait until the big rigs got right up to the turn-off and switch the scale sign from CLOSED to OPEN. Brakes would squeal, smoke. Truckers would swear, pulling their rigs around sharply. Night after night.

There were ten of them at the truck stop that night. Ten tired, fed up drivers. Rob looked at them. "If he pulls that stunt tonight I'm running the damn scale. Anybody with me?"

"Hell yes," they all said, laughing, keyed up.

Rob approached the scale slowly. CLOSED, flashed the sign. Just as he got to the turn-off it flashed again. OPEN. Rob gave a loud blast on the air horn and shot past the scale. The weigh master got in his little car and came after them. He passed the semi and pulled sharply in front of them. Rob let the truck roll and the little car carrying the weigh master was gently bumped off to the side of the road.

Randy looked at him wide eyed as they crossed the state line doing 80 mph. They could hear the sirens whining shrilly in the black distance. Rob pulled into the truck stop across the state line. Minutes later they were surrounded by police.

"Geez, Dad, what are we gonna do?"

Rob looked at him and grinned. "Well, I'm probably going to spend another night or two in jail. As for you, young man, you can stay here with the truck, or you can drive this load up to Harker's warehouse. It's only about a mile up the road and there's a little motel right next to the warehouse. You could stay there and wait for me if you'd rather do that. Do you have enough money?"

"Yeah, I've got plenty of money. But I think I better get this load up to Harker's. Don't want to mess up our reputation, you know, of always delivering on time. I'll wait for you at the motel."

Rob grinned, leaned over and messed up Randy's hair. "Be careful, son."

"No problem, Dad."

When Rob got out of the truck the police officers came toward him. Some of them had their hands on their guns.

"Hey, fellows," Rob said, easily. "I ran a scale. Didn't rob a bank.

Didn't shoot anybody. Just ran a scale. Now can we all kind of calm down here?"

"You also ran a weigh master off the road, mister. Lucky for you he wasn't hurt."

"Weigh master?" Rob asked, innocently. "That was the weigh master? Thought it was some old drunk. Pulled right in front of me…"

Two days and nights in the county jail. Four thousand dollars in fines. Randy. It cost him almost everything to run that scale.

CHAPTER EIGHT

Before the judge made his final decision he talked to Randy for a long time. He explained that both of his parents loved him but that his mother believed he would be better off if they moved away, if he wasn't allowed to see his father.

Randy looked down at the floor.

"What do you think, son?" the judge asked.

Randy wouldn't answer, wouldn't look at any of them.

Then the judge asked him about the last time he had gone with his dad. "Did he order you to drive that semi, son?"

Randy looked at him then. "No," he said, angrily. "What's the big deal about that anyway? I'm a good driver. As good as any man. Dad's said so lots of times. He asked me if I could handle it. He didn't make me drive the damn truck, I…"

Randy started to cry.

When it was all over, the judge decided that Randy's mother was right. Randolph Robert Townsend was given solely into the custody of the lady who used to be Rob's wife but wasn't anymore. She made plans to take the boy to Connecticut, to live near her family.

Rob tried to talk to him before he left. He didn't know what to say, how to say it.

"When will you come and see me?" the boy asked, voice small.

"I don't know, son. The judge says I don't have any visiting rights. I've got a lawyer working on it. I'm trying to get it changed."

"How come you're letting this happen?" Randy asked angrily. "Please do something, Dad," he said, tears in his eyes. "I don't want to leave you."

Rob held him close, the way he used to when he was little. "Do you think I haven't thought about just taking you, getting the hell out of here? You think I haven't thought about it?" Rob's own voice was becoming angry. He took Randy roughly by the shoulders. "You know what that would mean? You'd never see your mom again. Do you want that? Can you live with that? We'd be hiding out. I don't know what the hell to do, don't know whether to let you walk out of here and try to get it changed or throw you in a truck and run."

Rob turned away. "I love you. Don't ever forget that."

"I love you too," Randy said.

He left then, closing the door softly behind himself.

For a while after she left him, took the boy, took the very life out of him, he spent his time badly.

Rob was surprised to find out how easy it was to sit staring into an endless glass of beer, talking to other men, men who understood, men who held down bar stools instead of jobs, men who were beerily sympathetic. "Women. Damn women. Do it every time," they would say profoundly.

"Yeah," Rob said. "Damn woman. Shut me out. No love, couldn't touch her. Too damn high and mighty for that. Took my money all those years. Liked that well enough. Left me, took my boy, took Randy." Rob's voice slurred.

Self-pity was a seductive mistress.

His mother drove into town to see him. It was early morning, not yet eight. Rob was sitting at the kitchen table, unshaven, shirtless, working on his third beer.

"So?" she said, sitting down heavily in the chair next to his.

"So?" he repeated, grinning. He couldn't help it. He liked her, was glad she had come.

"How long, Rob?"

"How long what, Mom?"

31

"How long are you going to hide?"

"Hide? I'm not hiding. I'm right here for all the world to see. Good old Rob Townsend, super trucker, super dad, gold medal man, except I had to sell some of my trucks to pay for the divorce and I can't even see my son because I'm, I'm a bad influence on him. She really said that, said I was a bad influence on Randy."

"Right now I'd say she was probably right," his mother said, dryly.

Rob felt as if she had slapped him.

Her voice softened then. She reached out, covered his hand with hers. "It's not like you to give up like this. If you love Randy, love him the way I think you do, fight for him. Fight, Rob. Do what has to be done to change it. Even if you lose, it's important to try, important that Randy knows that you are trying. He needs to know he's important to you."

So he fought back.

The legal battle was a long one, long and costly. Rob sold all of the trucks except for Little Pete. He couldn't bear to part with him. He had been the boy's favorite.

One year later, when Randy turned seventeen, he had finally won the right to visit him, one weekend a month.

It was no good. Randy was lost to him, lost in politeness, in too much Connecticut proper.

Rob tried to reach him, tried to break through the wall of cool politeness the boy had built between them.

Randy didn't try.

The last time Rob had stopped by the university to see him, Randy had been busy, all tied up with friends.

Two paths. Mother. Father.

CHAPTER NINE

It was after nine when Rob finally got to Ghost Town. He pulled up to the fuel pumps, leaned back and lit up a cigarette. *Good old Ghost Town*, he thought lazily. *Full service fuel at self-serve prices. Nice. Especially nice on a cold night turning colder.*

He watched the fuel boy fumble around trying to get the fuel caps loosened up, glad to be inside Little Pete instead of out there freezing his hands off.

The boy climbed up the steps to wash his windows and Rob caught a glimpse of blue eyes and the boy's hood fell off and it wasn't a boy at all who was out there in the freezing cold washing his windows and filling his fuel tanks. It was some kind of incredibly beautiful woman.

Damn, I'd sure like to talk to this lady, he thought, opening the door. *Probably all a waste of time, probably married, got a three hundred pound mountain man for a husband.*

"Want some help?" he asked, lazily, leaning against the truck.

"No thank you," the woman said, politely.

"You married?" he asked.

"Am I what?" she asked, totally taken aback.

"Married," he said again, grinning. "You know like flowers and churches and long white gowns."

"Wh, why?" she stammered.

He grinned again. "Well, I was thinking about buying you a cup of coffee when you get off work. Then I was thinking maybe I

33

shouldn't because I kind of had this feeling you might be married and that your husband might turn out to be a three hundred pound mountain man and so…"

She laughed. "No, I'm not married. There's no," more laughter, "no three hundred pound mountain man but I'm…"

"Good," he said. "Then I'll consider buying you a cup of coffee."

"Consider?"

"Yep." He reached out, pulled her hood back up and gently tied it under her chin.

"See you. About eleven?"

She nodded.

My god, why did I just agree to have coffee with a trucker? Katie wondered as she watched him drive off toward the parking lot.

CHAPTER TEN

Katie walked into the restaurant a little after eleven and sat down at the trucker's table, pulling off scarves, gloves, coveralls. When she was quite finished, he smiled at her. "My God, you're beautiful." Then he grinned. "For a fuel boy that is."

"Thanks," Katie said. "I think."

"Rob Townsend," he said, holding out his hand.

"Katie, Katie O'Connor," she said, shaking hands with him.

"By the way," he said. "How in the hell did you get this job? You are one of the clumsiest fuel pump attendants I have ever seen."

"Well, I'm not really a fuel pump attendant. I sort of, well I guess I, I kind of run Ghost Town," Katie said, somewhat sheepishly.

Rob stared at her. "If you sort of, well ah, run Ghost Town what were you doing out there pumping fuel?"

Katie smiled. "Just the way I am I guess. I try to do a different job one day a week. I like to know what the people who work for me have to put up with, like," she added wickedly, "having strange men asking them if they're married and..."

"That bad, huh?" Rob asked.

"That bad," she said.

"Well," he said, leaning back in his chair, "that makes us about even. Here I thought I was having coffee with a hardworking, honest, clumsy laborer and you turn out to be the boss lady. Can't trust anybody these days. I'm glad I fell in love with you before I knew who you really were. That way we'll never have to worry that I just wanted you for your money."

Katie felt her cheeks get hot. *My God, I'm blushing*, she thought. *Stupid, he's just kidding around.*

She was about to respond when someone from behind her put two icy hands over her eyes.

Katie reached up, covered the small hands with hers.

"Jennifer?"

Jennifer slid her arms around Katie's neck and hugged her.

"Sit down, honey," Katie said. "Rob Townsend, Jennifer Davis."

Rob reached out, shook hands with Jennifer. "Howdy," he said.

"Hello," Jennifer said, smiling sweetly at him.

"How's it going?" Katie asked Jennifer.

"Not bad," Jennifer said. "I'm still working on your picture. I might have to have you sit for me again."

"No problem, honey. Just let me know. Are you hungry? Want anything from the famous Ghost Town kitchen?"

"No. No thanks. I saw you out at the fuel pumps and figured you'd still be around. I just wanted to say hi. I'm headed home now. I have to get up early tomorrow for Frank's class."

She gathered up her things, hugged Katie again, and left.

Rob looked confused and puzzled. "That beautiful little girl is, well she waited on me in the gift shop earlier, flirted wildly and kind of led me to believe that I just might get lucky tonight. Then a little later I saw her walking arm in arm with some young guy, heading for the trucks."

"I just hope the young guy she left with had long reddish hair and was wearing a cowboy hat," Katie said with a wan smile.

"Why would you hope that?"

"Because then she would be with Ben. He's a really good person, comes in every chance he gets to see her. She's been making better choices lately, I just hope, I, you see, Rob, I know all about Jennifer. That beautiful little girl you met in the gift shop is my niece."

The silence between them was long and uncomfortable.

Rob's dismay showed plainly on his face.

"Sorry," they both said at almost the same time.

They smiled at each other, feeling comfortable again.

"She's a beautiful girl, Katie."

"I know. She's beautiful, talented and more than a little mixed up. She looks fourteen but she turned eighteen this summer, legally an adult. I do what I can, love her, try to help, pray that she will be okay."

Katie gathered up her things. "Hey thanks for the coffee. It, it felt good to laugh," she added, holding out her hand.

Rob ignored her outstretched hand. "I'll walk you to your car," he said.

When they got to her jeep he leaned against the fender, looking intently at her. "Well here we are, ma'am. Time for us to make a very serious decision."

"What kind of decision?" she asked, puzzled. Then she grinned. "Surely we can wait a day or two before we decide anything about churches and flowers and long white gowns and..."

Rob laughed. "You've got a mean streak, lady. A real mean streak. Here I was just going to ask you about lunch tomorrow. About who's buying. Now seeing as how I bought your coffee tonight."

"I'll buy," Katie said, happily.

He reached out and shook hands with her. "G'nite, ma'am," he said, tipping his hat.

CHAPTER ELEVEN

Jennifer was beautiful and Jennifer was her niece and Jennifer had spent far too many nights in too many trucks and there really wasn't a hell of a lot Katie could do about it.

She thought about going to court, about trying to force her to get help. She thought about it a lot but she was scared. Jennifer was a legal adult and Katie knew that if she put too much pressure on her she would just run.

So she loved her and spent time with her and hugged her close and told her she was wonderful. And she was wonderful, wonderful and beautiful, inside and out.

Katie loved her very much and she wished she had known, known years ago, when Jennifer was seven or eight or nine, known what was happening in the big, still house on the lovely tree shaded street in the lovely town of Winnetka, Illinois.

CHAPTER TWELVE

Randolph Robert Townsend was stoned out of his gourd and it was good. Jimmy was at the wheel, snapping his fingers, singing along to the tape. The Grateful Dead. God, they were still so awesome.

That had been some concert. Thousands of Dead Heads, lights, sounds, the high, high, high feelings. The manic mystery of modern music. It was all there in Randy's head.

Randy could hear the girls giggling in the back of the van, could hear Teddy's laughter. *Should go join them,* he thought. *Sink down. Hold me a babe.*

But it was so good where he was. Jimmy. The music, the crazy patterns of headlights darting past on the highway. Darting lights. Dizzy silliness. Randy laughed at the darting, dizzy lights.

Sudden darkness, white lines on asphalt, too dark and a curve and...

From the suddenly still blackness Randy saw new lights, lights that were coming closer and closer and straight ahead and wait, "Wait! Jimmy, stop! Stop, Jimmy, stop!"

The brakes on the van squealed loudly, squealed too late, squealed inside Randy's head, squealed until everything stopped and his head was filled with a soft noiseless fog.

Randy opened his eyes and looked around. The door on the driver's side was flung open, crumpled, and Jimmy wasn't, where was Jimmy, and somebody was crying, sobbing, in the back of the van. He heard sirens, far away sirens, and then somebody was trying to open his door. Their voices, faded, sank softly into the soft fog inside his head.

"This one was wearing a seat belt. Lucky for him."

Randy slipped back inside his head, inside the fog, slipped away, thought he heard his dad's voice, his dad's words.

> "Buckle up, little buddy.
> Time to go trucking."

"Dad?" Randy whispered. "Dad?"

They unsnapped Randy's seat belt and lifted him out of the van and Jimmy was all bent and twisted and lying there and Randy started to cry.

"It's going to be okay, son," one of the men said. "It's going to be okay." They gently laid him on a stretcher, carried him to the waiting ambulance.

CHAPTER THIRTEEN

Just before midnight, the first flakes of snow started to fall on Ghost Town.

TUESDAY
January 14, 1985

CHAPTER ONE

Headlights, snow and mountains, a lonely, black, early morning run.

"How much farther now, Brad?"

Brad took his eyes off the road and looked over at his wife. Her body was rigid, face pale, soft brown eyes fixed on the snow packed road. There was already at least eight inches of fresh snow on the interstate. The wind was whistling around the cab and the damn snow just kept coming. They were totally alone, no other trucks on the road, no snowplows, no nothing. Just them and the most god awful blizzard Brad had ever tried to drive in.

"Only about forty miles now, Sandy. You scared, huh? Why don't you climb in the sleeper and close the curtains, close your eyes. We'll make Ghost Town okay. Then we'll wait this storm out, roads clear up, we'll take this ole truck back to Tulsa and go home for the winter. Be good to be back on the reservation again, see Larry. Remember when we first took him to the reservation to stay with your mama? He says he's afraid of all the Indians. He's a Cherokee but he's afraid of the Indians. Crazy little guy, huh?" Brad laughed, remembering.

He talked on, talked his easy, rambling bullshit. Sandy relaxed slightly, smiled. In a few minutes she got up, went back to the bunk, and was soon fast asleep, breathing softly, deep in a quiet, peaceful place inside herself.

Brad always wondered where she went when she slept like that, slept so peacefully, quietly.

Sandy had been a slip of a girl when he had first met her some twelve years ago. Brad had been horseback riding out in the Arizona desert. It was a hot, but still bearable, early April day. He had seen nothing all day except for a few sidewinders and an occasional circling buzzard. Midafternoon he spotted what looked like a homestead and headed in that direction. As he came around a clump of mesquite, there she was, sitting in an old wooden tub, long black braid hanging over the side, big brown eyes looking at him.

A screen door slammed and a man walked out. "Howdy," he said. "Like to come in, get cooled off?"

Brad nodded, got off his horse and followed the man. He glanced over his shoulder and caught a glimpse of her shy smile.

Brad stayed all day, swapping stories with her dad, eating her mom's tortillas, stayed there until evening shadows crept up the walls of the house. As he was leaving, thanking her parents, she smiled at him, told him goodbye. Softly.

He saw her every day for the next three weeks, never left her again.

Sandy Morning Star, no longer a slip of a girl, a soft cushiony woman, a friend. She warmed him with her softness. Her gentle ways had taken away the bitterness, the hurt, of the other times, the other wife.

He would get them safely to Ghost Town. Then he would take her home as he did every winter. They would walk through snow covered, protective pines, breathing deeply of their scent. In the evening they would build a fire of pinion wood and in the morning, when they awoke, the good air would be coming down from the mountains.

CHAPTER TWO

Randy had been floating in and out of himself for hours. Sometimes he was in a white, quiet place. Sometimes brakes were squealing and windshield glass was crackling into a million tiny stars, stars that flew away into an infinite, empty blackness.

He floated up out of the white, quiet place and opened his eyes.

White sheets. Half-light. His right arm was hooked up to some tubes and junk. He stirred restlessly.

The figure sitting beside his bed got up and laid a cool hand on his forehead. Cool lips brushed his cheek.

"Randy, are you awake?"

"Mom? What happened to me, Mom? Where am I? Where's Jimmy? Teddy, is Teddy okay? Where's Jimmy, Jimmy?"

His voice rose, bordering on hysteria.

The cool hand pushed the hair off his forehead soothingly. "It's all right, Randy. You're in the hospital. Everybody is okay. Your friends are okay and you're going to be fine. Just rest now, dear, just rest."

Randy closed his eyes, floated.

Caroline got up and went down the hall to the nurse's station, her high heels clicking sharply on the polished floor.

"My son just woke up," she said. "He was very upset, worried about his friends. I don't think he's sure about just what happened.

I want it strictly understood that no one is to tell him that Jimmy is dead. Not now, not until I think he's ready to handle it. I want him told that his friends are alright."

"That's up to you, of course," the head nurse said, "but do you think that's really wise? It might make it harder."

Caroline cut her off. "As you said, it's up to me to decide that." She turned to leave.

"Mrs. Townsend?" the nurse called after her.

Caroline stopped abruptly. No one had called her that in years.

"I'm not Mrs. Townsend," she said, slowly, deliberately. "Randolph's father and I have been divorced for years. My name is Mrs. Lawrence, Mrs. Steven Lawrence."

"I'm sorry, Mrs. Lawrence," the nurse said. "I just wanted to suggest that you talk with our hospital social worker, Dan Baker. He's had a lot of experience with this kind of thing. He's especially good with young people."

"All right. Thank you," Caroline said. "I'll talk with him when he comes in."

She went back down the hall to Randy's room.

Mrs. Townsend, Mrs. Rob Townsend.

Was anything ever really over? It had been so many years, so many years divorced. And before the divorce, so many years of cold, self-inflicted distance.

His fault? Her fault? Who knows? Who cares? Does anybody really give a good god damn?

She had loved him once, hadn't she? Maybe. Maybe not. And what the hell was love anyway.

She had been seventeen when she met Rob, a seventeen year old poor little rich girl, floating around in a cloud of auburn hair, laughingly enjoying her special place in this very special world.

Her friends had dared her, said she'd never do it, never walk into that bar alone. She got out of the car, stuck her tongue out at them, waved, and disappeared into the too close darkness on the other side of the door.

Suddenly it wasn't fun anymore and it wasn't smart and someone was blocking her way back to the door, reaching for her, and then she heard a voice, a good, strong voice.

"Beth Ann! What the hell."

And although her name was Caroline, she knew the good voice was talking to her and she turned and saw him making his way towards her, talking, walking slowly, carefully towards her.

"Excuse me mister, my kid sister. Beth Ann, Mom is gonna have a fit, you showing up here," he said, grinning in an embarrassed way at the sullen faces. "Kid sister," he mumbled disgustedly, taking her arm, steering her toward the door.

He took her safely back to her friends, shook hands with her and turned to leave.

"Hey wait! Wait a minute," she called. "I don't even know your name."

He came back, grinned. "Thought you'd never ask," he said.

Caroline thought that she had never seen anyone as gorgeous as Rob in all her life. He was so different from the tame little boys who took her politely to movies and danced properly with her at the country club.

So different.

They were married a year later. They laughed and loved and rode the trucks together and the little girl in the cloud of auburn hair became a young woman. And she loved him very much.

Then the baby came. He was crazy about the boy and she thought it would all work out, thought he would stay home with her, hold her close, be there when the boy got sick, be there when she needed him.

Rob did try, once, but he couldn't stand being in one place for too long. He was in love with the road.

She cried and she begged him to please stay home and she hurt and she got angry and she wanted him so, but on her terms, her way. And she felt mean and selfish and spoiled, but she held her meanness close to her at night when she lay there, not sleeping, alone in their bed, held it close, tenderly, the way he had once held her.

Caroline took the money he made from his greasy old trucks and created her own world. A fancy house, smart clothes, the right friends. And when he came home, a grin on his face, cold beer in hand, grease on his shirt, she no longer ran across the room and held him close. The little girl in the cloud of auburn hair wanted that so, wanted to run to him, feel his arms close around her, wanted to rest her head on his chest, feel safe. But the woman, hair carefully styled, hairspray stiff, said no. The woman, face set in a perfect mask, under perfect make up, said something disapproving about the dirt he was tracking in on the new carpet and moved graciously, regally, into another room.

And when he lay beside her at night and reached for her, she turned from him, and she lay there silently, holding her meanness close, holding it tenderly as she longed, still, for him to hold her.

And she loved him so.

And the boy. The boy was so much like the man, tall, blond, with the same heart breaking grin. Caroline found herself distancing herself from him also, from the son she loved. She was polite, cool, proper, properly loving, properly attentive. She became a kind, distant, proper parent.

Her dreams bothered her. She kept dreaming about Rob, dreaming that he was holding her, touching her face. She would bury her face in his chest then, breathe deeply of his smell, wondering as she always had, how come he always smelled so good, fresh, even when he was filthy dirty from the filthy damn trucks he smelled good. Like summer sun. Winds.

And she would wake up troubled and look across at this new man in her life, the man she now called husband, sleeping peacefully in the twin bed next to hers. He was a good man. He came home every night. He dressed properly. He never embarrassed her in front of her friends. He was intelligent, witty, and kind and he never drank beer from a can. He drank martinis, very dry. Many nights he drank many too many of those very dry martinis and when he came to her and she smelled his smell it was the smell of an old man, an old man who drank too much.

That made her want to cry but she never did.

If she could leave, right now, and go back to Rob and not hurt anybody in the leaving, would she? She did not know. She had those damn dreams. She had all of this damn guilt. But no one ever knew. No one ever suspected a thing. It was all hidden, all concealed under the perfect mask of her perfect make up and her perfect manners and her perfect life.

Caroline looked down at the sleeping Randy.

When they called and told her Randy was hurt she wanted to call Rob, wanted him to come, to stand by her side, wanted them to be there together when their son woke up. The little girl in the cloud of auburn hair wanted so to call him, to hear that good, strong voice again, wanted to feel safe, protected. But the woman said no.

Caroline sighed, sitting down again by Randy's side. *It's just as well*, she thought. *Damn truck driver probably wouldn't have been home anyway.*

CHAPTER THREE

The shower's hot water was drumming on her back, running down her body.

Katie rinsed the soap off, humming, held her head back, let the water splash her face, laughed.

She turned the water off and stepped out, toweling herself, looking in the full length mirror, studying her naked body.

"Not bad," she said. "Not bad for an old lady of thirty-five."

She ran her hands down her belly, felt a stirring, an unaccustomed, almost forgotten feeling of warmth. Her nipples became hard and erect.

Katie snatched her bath robe off the hook and quickly covered herself up.

She sat down in the kitchen absentmindedly stirring a cup of coffee.

Rob. What was it about him? Blushing last night, now this morning, feeling things she hadn't felt since?

"Since Joe," she said softly.

Face it, Katie, you're attracted
to him.

No, no I'm not!

Yes you are. You were thinking
all kinds of things last night,

looking at his hands, wondering
how they would feel on your
face, in your hair.

Oh, you're just being silly. I'm
just happy, that's all.

Well, what about those warm,
hot feelings in your belly just
now, young lady? Stupid, and
I'm not so young anyway.

Katie felt so damn happy. "And I'm not so old either." she said,
jumping up. "Now what in the world am I going to wear today?"

CHAPTER FOUR

Katie drove carefully through Guardian, steering her jeep around the biggest drifts. The snow was still falling and the early morning weather man had said it was going to get worse before it got better.

When she got to Ghost Town, Katie took her morning coffee to the dining room, sat there, looking out the window at the blizzard. The fresh white blanket of snow was covering, shielding, the winter bare earth, clinging softly to the pines, to the tops of the hitching posts that ran along the front of the main building.

So strange, the twists and turns one's life took. So strange to be here, to be running a truck stop, strange when all she had ever wanted to do was to teach, to work with children.

She had been a teacher for a while, a very good teacher, but that all ended when Little Joe died. There were too many reminders in that kindergarten classroom, too many reminders of her son: Sarah's toothless grin, the way Billy cocked his head when he listened to a story, Lisa's solemn black eyes. Teaching hurt too much.

Katie began to dread her work, started drinking. She kept a bottle under her bed, could not get up without the cup of gin that she poured for herself each morning, poured with sweating, trembling hands. She filled her thermos carefully for the day, gin, a little coffee.

The children were afraid of her.

The principal called Katie into her office and told her she would have to take a leave of absence. Katie didn't care, she really didn't give a shit. Now she could stay home alone, now she wouldn't have to spoil her gin with all that damn coffee.

It was her dad who finally had the strength to do what needed to be done. He came to her house and sat there, eyes worried, voice firm. "You're goin' to the hospital, Katie O'Connor. Now you can go under your own steam, so to speak, or I can go down and sign some papers and have you committed. Which will it be, darlin'?"

"I'm not going to any hospital, just forget it, just go away and leave me alone," she said.

"So are you wanting to be committed then, darlin'?" he asked.

"I will never, ever, forgive you if you do that," she said, voice low.

"Better to have you hating me than to have you dyin'," he said. "We've had a little bit too much of that in this family."

A few hours later the police came and took her to the hospital.

Katie was there for a very long time, and for a very long time nothing mattered, nothing touched her. She had hurt too much for too long, and when she woke up one morning and found herself wrapped in a comforting grey bubble, she decided to stay there. She liked the bubble, liked its flat grayness, its silence, liked not feeling, not hearing, liked looking out at Them and seeing Them grey, grey like her bubble, fuzzy, far away. Grey, fuzzy, far away things could not touch her, could not make her feel.

She lived in her bubble for a long time. Then one early spring day, when the ice was breaking up in the mountain streams, and the tender willows were shooting up green, her dad brought Jeremy to see her. He stood there in the visitor's room, old eyes confused, engineer's hat clutched tightly in one hand, holding out one of his favorite marbles, wanting her to take it, to reach out, to break her lovely grey bubble. Katie felt herself getting angry. He was too close, too real, not grey and fuzzy and far away.

"Damn it," she yelled. "Damn it, go away, go away, old man. I don't want you and your stupid old marble, just go away."

Katie turned and ran from the room, hands over her ears, shielding herself from the sudden loudness of the sound her slippered feet made as she ran down the carpeted hallway.

The bubble never came back. She wanted it to, but it would not.

Jeremy came back. And one day, when they were all outside, and Jeremy was trying to show her dad how to hold the taws, how to shoot the marbles out of the circle he had drawn on a bare patch of lawn, she found herself kneeling beside them, found herself holding the taw in her own hand.

"Knuckle down, Katie," Jeremy said, smiling at her. "Knuckle down, skinny bone tight."

Katie found herself shooting, squarely, expertly, found herself hugging him, tears in her eyes. Quiet tears.

It was mid-summer when Katie left the hospital. Her parents drove slowly through Guardian, the small town they called home, drove slowly past tree shaded streets that seemed too bright, slowly down the sleepy main street that seemed too loud, loud as her slippered feet had been running down the carpeted hallway.

"What about it, darlin'? Feel like seeing Ghost Town today?" her dad asked.

Katie didn't know if she wanted to see it or not. Ghost Town had come into existence during the long months Katie had been in the hospital, had replaced her dad's old fuel stop, little restaurant. The old place had been a second home, a place she had grown up with. Still they seemed so proud of this Ghost Town, so eager for her to see it.

"I, I think I'd like that," she said, hesitantly.

They took her to Ghost Town, drove up to the place where their dusty old truck stop had been and there were lawns, lawns lush and green, lawns and cobblestone walks and pines and flowers and shake shingle soft buildings. A wide plank sidewalk ran along the front of the buildings. There were hitching posts, swinging doors, and a good feeling of peace, of welcome, of coming home.

"How do you like it?" her dad asked anxiously.

She looked at him and smiled. "I love it," she said.

Ghost Town Truck Stop. She still loved it so.

CHAPTER FIVE

Tuesday morning, almost time for Jennifer to come walking through his door, cheeks red from the cold and snow, an eager, happy light in her eyes.

Frank Latimer sighed, turned away from the window, grateful to be there, grateful for his life, for art, for Jennifer.

Frank had lived in Guardian for almost twenty years, had come to this remote place in his early thirties. He was a young artist then, burned out on fame, too many wives, too many drugs. Critics praise had turned to derision, but Frank, always brutally honest with himself, had known long before the bad reviews that the gift he had always taken for granted was slipping away, that if things didn't change he was in danger of losing it entirely, might never get it back.

So he left everything, his New York apartment, friends, the civilized, cultured art world. He wasn't sure where to go but he knew his very existence depended on leaving. Frank drove through state after state, always heading west. When his head had cleared a little he thought about Montana, about a trip his dad had taken him on, up in the mountains, fishing. He remembered the air and the stars and the smell of pine trees and decided to go back, go see if the air still smelled like pines, if you could really see millions of stars on a clear night.

Frank drove through at least thirty little Montana towns before he pulled into Guardian. Something about it felt right. He liked the tree lined streets, the big old houses, the red brick schools. A few weeks later Frank was the proud owner of one of those houses, a big old house sitting on a bluff, right up against the mountains, across the road from the red brick Guardian High School.

His gift came back to him, slowly. The people in town accepted him, knew in some vague way that he was famous, sometimes tried to talk him into teaching an art class at the high school, tutor a student. Frank always declined those offers, always until Katie O'Connor showed up on his doorstep with an armful of paintings that her niece had done. When Katie told him Jennifer was only seventeen, begged him to work with her, told him her story, Frank surprised himself by agreeing to have Jennifer come to his studio one day a week.

Now he knew his time with Jennifer was going to come to an end. So he stood there, staring out the window, wondering how to tell her, wondering how to convince this special young woman to leave Guardian, leave her Aunt Katie, and go to New York.

Jennifer was already working on her latest painting when Frank found her in the studio. He looked at the picture. "It's good, Jennifer, very good." Frank rested his paint stained hand briefly, gently on the top of her head. "Come see me when you finish up today, ok?

"Sure," Jennifer said. She smiled up at him, watched as he left to go back to work.

The painting was good, very good. Jennifer felt that, deep inside. She was working on a family portrait, Mother, Richard, and Little Jennifer. Little Jennifer was holding Richard's hand. Richard was smiling down at her. Her mother was in the background, far away, unfocused.

So many pictures.

By the time she was four, her magic marker pictures had depth, dimension. They were tacked all over the small apartment she and her mother shared. When she first started school, her drawings had lined the classroom walls.

Even when they moved into his house, into the big quiet house on the lovely shaded street in Winnetka, the pictures came, demanding to be let out. Those pictures never hung on the classroom walls. They were not sunshine and flower pictures.

Sometimes during those years she would go to her mother's room, show her the pictures she had made.

Her mother did not like the pictures.

"Paint a pretty picture,
Jennifer. Make the world
pretty. Paint a pretty
world, Jennifer."

"Paint a pretty world, Mother?" She stared at the picture, at her mother's face, floating in the misty background. "Damn you," she whispered. "Why did you let him hurt me? Why didn't you make him stop?"

She felt the tears well up inside, filling her eyes. She wiped them away angrily. "I'm not going to cry today," she said. "Not about you."

Jennifer put her things away and went down the hall to Frank's office. She loved this house, loved Frank's office. The whole place smelled of paint, canvas, sometimes a faint hint of pot. She remembered how hard it had been for Katie to convince her to meet Frank, how scared she had been when she first came here, smiled at the memory. From the first time Jennifer came to work in Frank's studio she felt like she was finally exactly where she was supposed to be, knew when he first shook her hand that she would be safe here, safe with Frank.

"Sit down, Jennifer," he said when she came in. "Want a cup of coffee or a coke or anything?"

"No thanks," Jennifer said, wondering why in the world Frank was acting so weird. If she wanted a coke or coffee, she just went to get it. "What's up?" she asked him.

Frank smiled at her. "How would you like to go to school?" he asked.

"School?" she asked, puzzled. "I told you when I first came here that I didn't want to go to school, that I just wanted to learn to paint."

"I know," he said, "but I'm talking about a special kind of school. How would you like to go to a very special, very prestigious art school in New York City?"

"What, what are you talking about?" she asked, voice trembling. "I, I haven't even finished high school yet."

"I know," he said gently. "The Academy knows that too. Remember those three paintings I asked you for at Thanksgiving? I sent them to the selection committee at the Academy. They want you to come, Jennifer. They'll give you free tuition and a living allowance.

"When you first came here and talked to me about taking art lessons and showed me some of your work, do you remember what I told you?"

Jennifer shook her head.

"I told you that I couldn't teach you to be an artist, that you were already an artist, that I could help you learn some techniques, technical skills. And I did. But I've taken you as far as I can. You've learned everything you can from me. That's why I sent those pictures to New York."

He got up from behind the desk and walked over to her. He took the letter of acceptance and put it in her hands. "They *want* you to come," he said again.

CHAPTER SIX

Katie looked at the clock. Noon and no Rob. Probably that had just been a lot of talk last night. Probably he got in his truck and drove off right after she left. Probably she would never ever see Rob Townsend again and probably that was quite all right with her and probably...

"Katie?"

Katie looked up and saw him standing in the doorway. She felt a foolish smile take possession of her face.

"Hullo," she said, happily.

He came across the room and sat down on the edge of her desk. "Ready for lunch?"

She nodded, too happy to talk.

"Are you buying me lunch here or did you want to go someplace else? They're talking about closing the interstate but I guess we could go into Guardian if you want to."

"Let's have lunch here," she said. "Then I want to take some food up to a friend of mine. When it snows I like to check on him, make sure he has enough to eat. He only lives about two miles from here. Want to come along?"

"Sure," Rob said. "All this sitting around can get pretty old. Besides," he added, smiling, "in case you haven't noticed, I kind of like your company."

The afternoon shadows were long when Rob and Katie finally

left Jeremy's cabin and headed back to Ghost Town. The snowstorm had gotten worse, the wind blowing so hard that when they opened the door to leave, snow swirled into the cabin, stinging their faces.

"You be careful now," Jeremy called. "Looks like this storm has turned into a real, old fashioned blizzard."

Katie waved to Jeremy, drove her jeep carefully down the little road.

"I'm glad you asked me to come along," Rob said.

"Really?"

"Yep, really. You know, you just keep impressing the hell out of me. You're a boss lady, drive a jeep, have somebody as special as Jeremy for a friend. I keep thinking there must be something kind of special about you. Can't figure out what though," he added, thoughtfully.

"You're terrible," Katie said, laughing. "Every time you say something nice about me you say something else and take it all back. That's terrible!

"You really liked him? Jeremy?" she asked.

Rob grinned. "I sure did. He's the nicest real-life ghost I've ever met."

Katie laughed. "So you've heard those stories. Crazy, but you know if you think about it, Jeremy usually makes his rounds right before dawn. Imagine seeing him materialize around a corner, that old coat flapping around his knees." Katie shook her head, laughed again.

They drove in silence then, comfortable in that silence.

When they got back to Ghost Town, got out of the jeep, Rob grabbed Katie's hand. "C'mon," he said. "Now I want you to meet a friend of mine."

Rob led her back through the rows of trucks, back through the drifts and wind, back to Little Pete. He opened the door, bowed, and helped her up the steps.

"Little Pete," he said, "I want you to meet Ms. Katie O'Connor. Katie, this is Little Pete, the best old truck on the road."

Katie looked around the cab. "He's beautiful, Rob, just beautiful. Like a little house. A very little house," she added, smiling.

Rob got up, walked over to her, took her hands in his, led her back toward the bunk.

Katie shook her head, backed away.

"I just want to hold you, that's all, just put my arms around you. C'mon," he said softly, pulling her down to sit beside him. Rob put his arms around her, his face in her hair.

They sat that way for a long time, silent. When Katie looked up at him, he smiled and kissed the tip of her nose. "Okay, ma'am?" he asked.

"Okay," she said.

"Still scared?"

She shook her head yes. Rob kissed the top of her head, leaned back against the wall of the bunk, lit up a cigarette, grinned. "I'm not really a very scary person," he said. "Kind of meek and mild mannered and shy."

She smiled. "Bullshit," she said.

He raised one eye brow. "Truth," he said, still smiling.

Katie started talking, words tumbling out, telling him about Joe, Little Joe. She wanted him to know it wasn't him, wanted him to know how she felt about him, how much she wanted him, how scared she was.

"I, I want you so, Rob," she said softly. "I haven't wanted anybody in such a long time, haven't had these feelings, felt this way, not since, since Joe, and I'm so scared and I don't even know what I'm scared of." She stopped, tears in her eyes.

He put his arms around her. "It's okay, Katie. It's okay."

CHAPTER SEVEN

Jeremy was glad they had come. He loved Katie and he had liked Rob, liked the way he smiled. He liked having them in his house but their leaving had left him feeling a little lonely, a little sad. He looked out at the already deep snow. *Squirrels will be hungry. Birds too,* he thought.

Jeremy pulled on his boots, his old overcoat, and went out to check the feeders.

Two ground squirrels chattered noisily at him, sticking their heads out of a snowy burrow. The winter birds scattered at his approach, flying onto the branches of the nearby trees. Jeremy filled all of the feeders and headed up the steep hill toward the stream. He wondered how it would all look in the fresh snow with the rocks and the swift blue icy water and there was a little puppy sitting there, sitting right in his path, shivering.

"What are you doing, little dog?" he asked. "You lost? I bet you're hungry, huh?"

He picked the puppy up and took her back to the cabin. He could always check on the stream tomorrow.

"You like pork chops?" he asked the puppy. "Katie brought us some pork chops. Think we should eat some, get you warm. You're just a little girl. What else? Milk? Milk would be good for you."

Jeremy watched the puppy eat, happy to have found a new friend. "What's your name, little dog? What'd you think? You like Kim? Want me to call you that? Call you Kimber? That's a good name.

"You stay with me for a little while, stay and stay if you want to. Pretty soon, when the snow stops, we'll go see Ghost Town, make a circle."

CHAPTER EIGHT

Fifteen miles to go, twenty at the most, and he wasn't going to make it. If he were loaded, if that damn box behind him was carrying forty thousand pounds of freight, carrying something, anything except thin air, he could inch his way in.

Dan checked his mirrors, saw the high, empty trailer swinging out again, coming around to say hello to him. "Damn," he said, "damn it all."

He accelerated and stayed in front of it, got it back where it belonged, and looked for a place to pull over.

Dan found a wide place in the road and pulled the semi over next to a high, snow covered bank. He pulled out the airbrakes and felt his tight muscles start to loosen up.

He played with the CB, hoping against hope that it would work. He had been having trouble with it ever since he left Seattle, but the load he delivered earlier was a hot one and he had not taken the time to get it fixed.

Oh well, Dan thought, *no big deal. Somebody will come along pretty soon and I'll catch a ride into Ghost Town, call Edie, come back for the truck after the roads are clear.*

He leaned back and lit a cigarette, feeling pretty damn good really, feeling glad he hadn't wrecked the darn thing, gone over a mountain someplace. Empty semis and snow were a bad combination and this was about the worst storm he had ever been caught in.

Dan was just sitting there, all relaxed and lazy feeling, when he heard a deafening rumble and felt the truck shake. Seconds later everything went black. It took him a little while to figure out what had happened. The snow on the mountain had broken loose and come down over the bank, burying the semi. He was buried alive in a damn semi, buried under a mountain of snow in the middle of nowhere.

The tip of Dan's cigarette, glowing bright in the sudden darkness, was trembling, shaking, as his hands were shaking.

The panic hit him then. He fought it down. He turned the dome light on and felt somewhat steadied, reassured.

Dan heard the steady drone of the big engine, checked his gauges, and started talking loudly to himself.

"Got plenty of fuel. Almost full. 150 gallons. Gallon an hour? Gives me 150 hours before I start to freeze.

Smoke stacks clear? Must be. Be okay if she don't freeze up on me. Don't think about that, old man. Stacks clear, maybe they'll see the smoke, find me.

If they're looking. They're looking, or will be. Edie doesn't hear from me by tomorrow she'll be on that phone. Thank God for a worrying woman.

Now, if I can just, just hold onto myself. Don't do it, old man, don't give into it, not now."

Seventy-two year old Dan Collier got up and went back to his bunk to check his supplies. *Plenty of food and water. Carried the damn stuff around every year for forty years. Never needed it before, sure need it now.*

Dan was a good man, a good trucker. He kept talking about quitting but he never quite got around to it.

> Just one more run, honey. Ed
> wants me to haul this load
> out to L.A. for him.

Just one more run.

CHAPTER NINE

The beer was all gone. The bottles of piss had been dumped into a garbage can and Abraham had gotten a shower. His beard, a beard of several weeks' growth, had been removed. Abraham was wearing polished boots, a white shirt, a fine black suit.

Abraham did not know how long he had been drunk, did not know for sure how long he had been in Ghost Town. All he knew was that he was hungry, really hungry for the first time in days. He went into the dining room, found an empty table, ordered bacon, eggs, and a pot of hot coffee. The dining room was busy, even in the middle of the afternoon.

The storm, Abraham thought, *they're here to wait out the storm.*

He watched as a man and a woman came in, looking around for a table. "You all are welcome to join me," Abraham said. "I'm just working on a late breakfast here. Just came in from Bozeman" he said, the lie rolling easily off his tongue. "Roads are mighty bad, mighty bad."

"Just came down that way myself," the guy said. "You're right about those roads. I heard they just closed the interstate. Here, Sandy, sit down," he said, motioning to the woman. "We'll eat with this guy here. I'm Brad, but they call me the Cherokee Kid and this is Morning Star. What's your handle?"

Abraham shook hands with the two of them. "They call me Preacher Man," he said humbly.

❖◆❖◆❖

The summer Abe was twelve, HE brought Abe a fine black suit, black like HIS own. HE took the suit up to the boy's room.

"You're almost a man now, boy. A man needs a suit to wear for the Lord's work. You're gonna have many temptations now, boy, many temptations. Girls, scarlet women, all wanting a fine young man to lay with them.

"You laid with a woman yet, boy?" HE asked, voice gentle.

Abe felt his cheeks flush. "No, sir," he said, looking at the floor.

"Look at me when you speak, boy." Thunder and Lightning.

"Yes, sir," Abe said, looking up at HIM. "I been clean for you, sir, for the Lord," Abe said proudly.

Brother Michael, looking unaccustomedly embarrassed, patted Abraham awkwardly on the shoulder. "Put on your new suit, son, I'll be waiting for you downstairs."

Abraham's Mama made a big to do about his new suit. HE smiled his approval and gave Abe fifty cents to spend at the corners store.

Abraham knew every step of the way to the store, had been running down that road, barefoot since forever.

Tonight was different. He wasn't a little boy anymore, a little boy who followed a Preacher Man around. He was someone else tonight, not boy, not man. Abraham was somewhere in between, in between Preacher Boy and Preacher Man.

Preacher Man. A fine black suit. Thunder and Lightning.

They were waiting for him down the summer dusty road. Three of them: Skeeter, Billy and Matt. Abraham had known them, as he had known everyone in his little world, since forever.

"Where you goin', Preacher Boy?" Matt asked.

"That's no Preacher Boy," Skeeter said, mock surprise in his voice. "That there's a real, honest to God Preacher Man. Why he's got a fine black suit and..."

Skeeter and Matt grabbed his arms, held him fast. Billy shoved his face in Abe's, shoved it so close that Abe felt dizzy, from fear, from the unaccustomed stench of corn liquor.

"You think yer so high and mighty, so holy. Here, have some fire water, Preacher Boy. Prepare you for hell." Billy took the jug, forced Abe's mouth open, poured the raw, hot liquid down the boy's throat. Abraham doubled over, choking.

"Have another snort, Preacher Boy," Billy said, forcing the jug on the boy again.

"You think Brother Michael's such a fine man, such a wonder. Time you got educated, boy. Brother Michael, he's nothing but a randy old billy goat dressed in God's clothes. You know what he's doin'? Right now? With your fine Mama? Know why he sent you to the store? They prayin'? Prayin'? Hell, I'd like to pray like that. You know what he's doin'?" Billy demanded.

Abraham shook his head no, felt all dizzy inside. He struggled, wanting to be free, to be walking down the road alone in his fine black preacher's suit.

"Let's just show him," Matt suggested.

"Yeah," Skeeter said. "Time you see what he's really like."

They drug him back to the house, their voices hammering in his ears.

> You know what a randy old billy goat does? Sticks his thing in any hole he can find. He gets em all hot with his fine Preachin'. Little girls. Fine women. Gets em hot. Cools em down.
>
> Why you think so many babies born after he's been here? You one of them babies, Preacher Boy? You look just like him.

He bugger you yet, Preacher Boy? He
bugger me when I was just twelve.
Said it was the Lord's instrument,
said, oh shit…

Billy was crying. Their voices subsided as they neared
Abraham's house. They took him up to the window and pushed his
face against the glass. For a moment Abraham could see nothing.
Then he saw them on the floor, naked bodies intertwined. HE was
naked. HE was rutting Abe's Mama, like Abe had seen dogs, bulls,
billy goats do, since forever. The instrument of the Lord, fine strong,
in his fine Mama.

Randy old billy goat.

Babies. You one of them babies?

Little girls. Fine women like yer fine
Mama.

He bugger you yet boy, bugger you yet
boy, bugger you.

Abraham threw up, upchucked, right outside the window.
They pulled him away into a nearby grove of pine trees. "Time
you knew the truth, Preacher Boy," Skeeter said, passing him the
jug of corn liquor.
"Drink up, Preacher Boy," Billy said. "Make you feel better."
Abraham raised the jug to his lips and drank deeply. "Whore,"
he said, bitterly. "My fine Mama is nothin' but a whore."

CHAPTER TEN

Jennifer sat silently in her room, holding the letter, not able to look at it, read it, make it real.

When she finally read the words, words that said she had great promise, that they were looking forward to working with her, she was unable to contain herself. She threw on a coat and went to find Katie.

Jennifer ran out to her rusty VW, coat flying behind her. *Just get me to Ghost Town,* she thought, patting the old dashboard.

When she got to Ghost Town, Jennifer breathed a sigh of relief. She had barely made it. If she was going to get her car back home, she'd have to have the mechanics put chains on her tires.

Jennifer ran inside and opened the door to Katie's office.

"Katie?"

"Hi, honey," Katie said. "Come on in. How was class this morning?"

Jennifer didn't say anything. She walked across the room and handed the letter to Katie.

Katie took the letter, read it, read it again. "My God, Jennifer, you're going to New York."

She jumped up and gave Jennifer a hug, holding her close. Then she stood back, looked at her. "You're going to New York, to art school, you're going to be a famous artist."

Katie hugged her again, whirled her around. Jennifer's eyes were shining. "We have to do something to celebrate," Katie said.

"Let's go down to, oh shit, I forgot about the roads. We can't really go anywhere, can we? Come on," Katie said.

She grabbed Jennifer's hand and pulled her along to the dining room. "Sit here," Katie ordered. Katie disappeared into the kitchen and came back shortly, carrying a big cake. The cake had CONGRATULATIONS JENNIFER written across the top.

"This is the best I can do on short notice," Katie said. "As soon as the snow stops, and the roads are open, we'll go to Bozeman, shop for some school clothes for you, go to Marios for dinner."

Jennifer looked at the big cake, laughed. "If we eat all of this I won't fit in any school clothes."

"We'll share," Katie said. One of the waitresses brought over some plates and Katie and Jennifer passed pieces of cake around the dining room.

Jennifer took some cake over to Abraham's table.

"What's happening?" Brad asked her.

"I got a scholarship to go to an art school in New York. I just found out about it today," Jennifer told him.

"That's good," Sandy told her. "I'm happy for you."

"Thank you," Jennifer said.

"Did you want some cake, sir?" she asked Abraham. Abraham looked up at her. His eyes were blue. He had blue, cold, icy eyes, eyes like ice, like...

Jennifer set the plate down, not waiting for an answer. *Stupid,* she told herself. *You don't have to be afraid now. He's not Richard, just his eyes, hard, cold, not Richard. You don't have to be afraid. He's not Richard.* She sat back down with Katie and started working on a big piece of cake.

Outside the wind blew, whistled around Ghost Town, the snow continued to fall. Inside, sitting with her Aunt Katie, Jennifer felt safe again, knew that Katie would give her a ride back to her apartment, knew that she didn't have to be afraid of cold, icy eyes tonight.

CHAPTER ELEVEN

Her little apartment was warm and safe. She got ready for bed slowly, washed her face, brushed her teeth, her hair, just as Richard had taught her to do when she was Little Jennifer.

"And this is Little Jennifer," he told the nurses in his office, holding her hand.

"My, what a beautiful little girl, Dr. Warren."

"Lucky little girl to have a new Daddy like you, Dr. Warren."

Just like a little princess. A pretty little princess. Little Jennifer. Lucky Little Jennifer.

Little Jennifer finished brushing her hair. "Where's my mommie?" she asked him.

"Your mommie's asleep."

"How come she's asleep? How come she doesn't read to me anymore?" Little Jennifer's eyes filled with tears.

Richard took her hand and led her to her room. Big house. Quiet house. Mommie was asleep.

"Here, Little Jennifer, here now. Let me see. Yes, you can wear these pretty little PJ's to bed. Pretty little PJ's. Pretty Little Jennifer."

He pulled her little panties down. Near dark. Hot breath.

"Mommie! I want my Mommie!"

Icy eyes. "Quiet!"

Little Jennifer was quiet.

He lifted her up on his lap. "Jennifer. Pretty Little Jennifer," he sang. He put her in bed and tucked her in.

Sometimes he came back. Later.

"Mommie! Mommie he's hurting me. Mommie! Mommieee..."

Jennifer looked at herself in the mirror. "Stop!" she said, firmly. *I'm not Little Jennifer anymore and I don't have to be afraid.*

Maybe when she went to school she wouldn't have to hate anymore.

WEDNESDAY
January 15, 1985

CHAPTER ONE

The tubes in his arm were gone. The fog inside his head was gone. His mom was gone. Randy was ready to be gone, ready to leave, goodbye hospital.

"Randy?"

Randy looked up and saw a man standing in the doorway. He was wearing a sports coat and dress slacks. *Social worker, psychologist, maybe both?* Randy wondered.

"Dan Baker," the man said, offering his hand.

"Which one are you?" Randy asked, shaking his hand.

"Which what?" Dan asked, sounding puzzled

"Psychologist or social worker?"

"Ohhh," Dan said, smiling. "Social worker."

Randy looked at him appraisingly. "Are you the one they hired to tell me the truth?" he asked.

"The truth?" Dan asked.

"About Jimmy. He's dead isn't he?"

"Yes, he's dead, Randy. I'm sorry."

"Why in the hell did she lie to me?"

"She was worried about you. Don't be too hard on your mother. A lot of people have a hard time dealing with death."

"I know, but why couldn't she just tell me the simple truth for once? Always makes everything unreal, keeps everything so damn pleasant, so... I knew Jimmy was dead, knew it when I saw him lying there on the damn road, saw him, like I saw that semi driver when I was just a little kid."

A voice on the CB, urgent, repetitive. "Injury accident. Trucker in need of assistance. Injury accident. Police and ambulance assistance needed. Injury…"

Seven year old Randy rubbed the sleep out of his eyes and sat up, looking around for his dad. "Dad? Dad?" Randy climbed out of the cab and ran barefoot down the side of the road. He saw them standing there. His dad, two or three other drivers, saw another man lying on the grass. The man on the grass was all broken and twisted and...

Randy slipped his hand inside his dad's. Rob looked down at him.

"Is, is he dead, Dad?"

"Yes, he's dead."

They stood there silently, waiting for the ambulance to arrive.

"Dad talked to me about that guy dying. I know about death. He says, says death is as much a part of life as being born. Says we hide it now, make it scary, unreal. Hire professionals to handle the remains. Shit. Now they hire professionals to tell people about it."

Randy looked restlessly around the hospital room. "Hey, no offense, but I really want to get out of here, okay?"

"Are you going to be all right?" Dan asked.

"Yeah, I'll be okay."

"Listen," Dan said, handing him one of his cards. "Sometimes things like this can get people down, really down. If that happens, you give me a call. My number is on the card I gave you. You give me a call and we'll talk. Okay?"

"All right," Randy said. "Thanks."

They shook hands. "You know, you're not too bad," Randy said. "For a social worker that is."

CHAPTER TWO

Jimmy was dead.

Everybody else was okay. Teddy, the girls, the couple in the other car, all okay.

Not Jimmy. Jimmy was dead.

Jimmy was the first friend Randy had when he came east, a confused young Texan transported unwillingly to this land of Connecticut Yankees.

His stomach hurt all the time then. He walked alone, lay alone at night in a strange room she said was his, lay curled up, staring, not seeing, feeling small and isolated, feeling alone.

He walked to school alone, walked the halls smelling of wax, alone.

Randy didn't know who he hated the most. Her, for taking him away, him, for letting it happen, for standing there, big hands hanging helplessly at his side. Shit. Big man. His dad. His hero. Shit.

He was walking home alone one day when someone tackled him from behind. Randy landed heavily on the sidewalk. He rolled quickly to one side, springing to his feet, fists ready.

The boy who had tackled him was crouched in the grass, laughing. "Hey, man, just saved your life. Duck! Duck, man!" he said, ducking low, covering his head with his arms in mock terror. "Shit, here they come again, flying saucers, Greeley Monsters," ducking again, rolling in the grass with laughter.

Randy smiled and sat down on the sidewalk. "You're nuts," he said to the boy. "Crazy. Certifiably crazy."

"I know," the boy said, "but I'm a good kid. Heard my mama say so just last week. Name's Jimmy, Jimmy Baxter." He held out his hand.

Randy took the outstretched hand, grinned. "Randy. Randy Townsend," he said.

Jimmy Baxter was dead.

CHAPTER THREE

Katie had arrived at her office early, hoping to get a head start on the mounting pile of paperwork that was lying on her desk.

Instead, she found herself sitting there, staring at the pile of papers, lost in thought.

What in the hell is the matter with you? Staring off into space is not your style, Ms. O'Connor. I'm not staring off into space. I'm. Dreaming? Yes, I guess so.

Dreamily.

CHAPTER FOUR

Abraham finished his breakfast and headed back to his truck. The interstate was closed, the drifts were getting deeper and deeper and the god damn snow just kept coming down. It was starting to get to him, the snow, the cold, the staying in one place. He felt a familiar dark, tense anger building up inside himself.

He wanted to get in his noisy old Freightliner and take off, drive for twenty or thirty hours, pedal to the metal, window rolled down, wind in his face.

Driving helped.

If only he could hit the road, plug in one of his tapes, sing along, loudly, tonelessly. The words to "Freightliner Fever" played over and over through his head.

Abraham wanted to feel that terrible tiredness again, the kind of tired that would let him sleep dreamless, demonless.

Sometimes, when he was driving late at night, West Coast turn around high, he saw demons in his mirrors, disembodied demons with Cheshire Cat grins, black burning sockets where the eyes should have been. The demons in his mirrors did not frighten him. He had been suckled on worse. Abraham would throw his head back and laugh, shouting HIS words into the wind.

> "And I saw a beast rising out of the sea, with ten horns and seven heads, with ten diadems upon its horns and a blasphemous name upon its heads."

And the demons in the mirrors grinned their headless grins and laughed with him.

If only he could leave this place.

Abraham climbed over the doghouse to his bunk, dug around through the pile of dirty clothes, looking for his bible. He would read a few verses. Maybe that would help to quiet the pounding in his head.

He ran his hand around the sides of the mattress and his fingers found something hard and cold and small. Abraham pulled it out, felt the pounding inside quicken.

A small gold locket.

A picture.

Mama.

Long blonde hair. Little girl's
face.

Abraham's fine mama.

Mama. High lace collar. Mama,
sitting straight as an arrow on
the hard church pew.

Mama. Proud walk, head held
high. A fine lady.

Mama. Little girl hands brushed
the hair off his forehead. Soft
lips brushed his cheek. "Sleep
tight, Little Abraham."

Mama. His fine Mama, naked,
rolling around on the floor.

Mama. His Mama was a whore.
Wanton. A scarlet woman.

HE was above reproach and hatred. HE was the Preacher Man. HE had been made weak as all men were weakened, by soft, yielding flesh, by lips, "Lips that drip as an honeycomb."

Abraham snapped the locket shut. "Why, Mama? Why?"

Abraham lay down in the sleeper and pressed his hands against his temples. The pounding was getting worse. It was her fault, all her fault.

CHAPTER FIVE

Jennifer walked happily through the deep snow, gloved hands deep in the pockets of her old denim jacket. They still hadn't plowed the streets in Guardian but no one seemed to mind. They were used to blizzards in this part of Montana.

When Jennifer first arrived in the little town, she couldn't see how anyone could live with the isolation, the extremes in the weather. Now she liked to walk through town, saying hello to people who knew her name, people who seemed to like her, care about her. *Guardian. A good name for a little mountain town. A good name for a safe place.*

By the time she got to the bank her cheeks were flushed with the cold and her soft hair was covered with an even softer cap of snow. She liked the little bank, liked it when they called her Jenny, called her honey.

She went to Mary Kelly's window, told her she wanted to check on the balance in her saving's account. Mary started talking nonstop, eager for news about Ghost Town.

"I bet the restaurant at Ghost Town is super busy these days," she said. "I suppose those truckers are getting anxious to be back on the road. Have you heard anything about the interstate? I can't remember when it was ever closed for this long."

Jennifer laughed, not sure what to respond to first. "Yeah, we are busy but I think most of the truckers are glad they're stuck at Ghost Town instead of some other god forsaken truck stop. I don't know about the interstate. Katie said they pulled all of the snow plows off the roads last night. Too dangerous I guess."

Mary smiled, patted Jennifer's hand. "You be careful going over there in this storm."

"Thanks," Jennifer said, "I will." She stared at the slip of paper with her account balance. It wasn't a lot but it would be enough. If it wasn't, Katie would help her out. No more men, no more money, not now.

Not that kind of money.

When she was little, it was new dolls, teddy bears, ice cream sodas and trips to the zoo. When she got a little older he would slide a fifty under her door, put a hundred dollar bill in her blouse pocket. Richard paid well for his pleasures.

Sometimes Jennifer had made THEM pay well too, for their pleasures. And every time she put the money in her pocket she felt a little kick, a mean little sense of satisfaction. Like evening the score…a little.

No more. Not now. Jennifer Davis was never going to use men that way again. Jennifer Davis was as artist. Jennifer Davis was going to school. That seemed so strange to her. She had not been inside of a school for a long time, not since her mother died and left her all alone with him.

The day after her mother's funeral she walked slowly down the lovely shaded street toward school. When she got to the big brick building with the lovely green campus she kept on walking.

Jennifer had $640 in her pocket. She hitched a ride with a trucker at the edge of town. He was lonesome and kind of fat and not too bright, but his eyes weren't icy and he bought her dinner and took her as far as Shreveport, Louisiana.

After that, she picked out other men, other truckers. She thought a lot during those long rides in those noisy, often dirty trucks: about her mother, Richard. She thought about her Aunt Katie too, about how kind she was, about how she had asked her to come and live with her when her mother died. Two months after she left Winnetka, left Richard, Jennifer wandered into the Ghost Town Truck Stop and knocked on her aunt's door.

Jennifer loved her Aunt Katie but she was not about to get too close to anybody. She politely refused to move in with her aunt. She got her own apartment, fixed her own meals, took art classes, painted, and in the evenings she worked in the big gift shop at Ghost Town. She took a small, mean pleasure in flirting with the truckers, liked to see them sweat with wanting her. Sometimes she would pick one out, go with him to his truck, climb in his bunk. She hadn't done that for months, not since she'd met Ben, Big Ben she called him, big and gentle with kind, brown eyes. Now she was going away. Jennifer Davis was going to school.

CHAPTER SIX

Jeremy sometimes wondered how old he really was. He didn't know for sure and his family was all dead so they couldn't tell him. He figured he must be pretty old by now, maybe even in his nineties. Ninety years old maybe. That was pretty old he guessed. He didn't feel old today, he felt like a little kid.

Jeremy pulled on his boots, opened the cabin door and went outside to play in the still falling snow. The snow was too cold and dry to pack. No snowman could be molded today. Jeremy lifted his old knees high and tramped around in front of his cabin. He was making a circle, making it the old way, for the old game. A circle, tracks, the old game, the old way. The fox and geese game. Jeremy could hear their voices: Lisbeth, Matt, Daniel, Mary Jo, the voices of his childhood. Country school, the circle, his knees didn't hurt then. He could run, he was strong, he was swift, he was...the FOX!!

The teacher was young that year. She had kind eyes.

Little Jeremy no longer cried when it was time to go to school but he still walked slowly, solemnly along, marking time, storing up things, things like the sky, the wind, the shadows on the sun. Jeremy stored them up carefully, kept them inside, to keep him safe while he was in school.

She understood. She gave him a special place by the small window. On warm days she opened it wide for him, stopping to look at his pictures, touching him lightly on the back of the head as she walked past.

She understood. She never made his head hurt with letters and numbers. She spoke slowly, softly, just to him. He did not have to stand up in front of the others, stand up stammering, feeling ashamed. He did not have to go to the blackboard and work his sums. He could do that slowly, carefully, at his special place by the window. And they started to make sense to him, the strange letters and numbers. He played games with them, his games, drew them carefully, colored them red, white and blue.

Sometimes the other children complained. "How come Jeremy doesn't have to come up to the blackboard? How come Jeremy always gets to sit by the window?"

"How come?"

"Hush," she would say. "We all have special things in us, special ways of learning. Jeremy has a special need to be close to the outside. That's his special need, his special way of learning." She looked around thoughtfully. "Now Johnny, Johnny learns best if he sticks his tongue out of the corner of his mouth when he's thinking. And Lisbeth, Lisbeth, you learn best when you twist your braid round and round your fingers and..." She paused, "Now, shall we cut off Johnny's tongue? Lisbeth's braid?" Laughter. "No? Then I don't think we should cut off Jeremy's window either."

The children learned to understand and they learned to laugh with him, not at him. Some of them started walking home with him and they learned to see the hills, the sky, in his special way.

One soft, warm, winter's day, after the teacher and the other children had all gone home, Jeremy and Lisbeth went behind the school house to play. They ran round and round the snowy circle, falling down, laughing.

"Got to go now, Lisbeth," Jeremy said, looking at the sky. "Time for this old FOX to be going home."

Jeremy walked around the corner of the school house, hands in his pockets, whistling softly. He had maybe stayed too long but he was sure a good fox, sure could run, catch those old geese.

They grabbed him then, three big boys, boys who had left school years ago.

"Where you think you're
going, Dummy?"

"Like the snow? Here,
want some?" rubbing a
fistful in his face.

Jeremy didn't fight. He
didn't know how.

"Chicken. Dumb little
chicken shit."

They picked him up by his arms and carried him over to the outhouse. They put him inside the small, dark building and locked the door, barring it with a strong wooden plank.

It was very dark inside, dark and close and scary and there was no light and no air and Jeremy felt like he couldn't breathe, couldn't...

After the big boys were gone, Lisbeth called to him and tried to get the door open but the big wooden plank was too heavy.

"Jeremy? Jeremy!" Lisbeth called.

He didn't answer her, just whimpered.

"I know, I'll go get the teacher. Jeremy, I'm gonna go get the teacher," she said.

When they got back to the school and the kind young teacher got the door open, Jeremy was lying on the floor of the outhouse. He didn't move when they opened the door.

"Is he dead, teacher?" Lisbeth asked, eyes big and scared.

"No, no Lisbeth, he's not dead. Just scared I think." She lifted him up in her arms and carried him out of the cold, dark outhouse. She sat down in the school yard, cradling the little boy in her arms. Jeremy sat up then and reached out to touch the snow, tears running down his cheeks.

"Inside dark scares me, teacher. Scares me bad," he said.

CHAPTER SEVEN

T he papers lay there, untouched, on her desk. A whole day had slipped away from her.

Katie felt sad and lonely, ridiculously, nonsensically lonely. How could she be lonely for someone she hardly knew? If he was messing up her mind this badly in just a few short days what would happen to her if this went any farther? What if they made love and he just drove away when the roads were clear, drove away and left her here all alone? Could she handle that?

Katie had expected him to come wandering into her office sometime during the day but he hadn't. She had even made several trips to the dining room, ostensibly on business, but she wasn't fooling herself. She had been looking for Rob.

Maybe he was angry with her, maybe...

So what's the matter? Are you trapped in some time warp? This is the eighties. You don't have to sit here and wait and worry. You could walk out to his truck. Knock on his door.

Yes, but what if he doesn't want to see me? If he wants to see me why hasn't he come in here?

Maybe he's thinking the same things, maybe he's thinking hey, if

she wants to see me why doesn't she
come out here?

Rob? Thinking that? He has to know
I like him. Really? How? You spent
the entire evening talking about Joe.

Only thing he probably knows is that
you love Joe. You don't really think
that, do you?

Lisa poked her head in the door. "Rob Townsend to see you, Katie."

Katie felt that foolish smile take possession of her face again.
She stood up and met him halfway across the room.

"I thought you were mad at me, that you didn't want to see me
anymore."

Rob tipped her chin up and looked sternly down at her. "I've
been thinking about you all day. I was thinking about just staying
the hell away from you. What do I need this for? If the roads were
open I probably would have just driven off." He grinned. "And
then twenty miles down the road I would have turned around and
come back."

Katie reached up and touched his lips.

Their first kiss was long and warm and felt like forever and
somewhere, far away, the phone was ringing."

"I have to answer that," Katie mumbled.

Rob let go of her and went to sit on the edge of her desk.

"Hello. Yes this is the manager. Can I help you? When was
your husband supposed to have gotten here, Mrs. Collier? Really?
Yes I know you're worried. Listen, we'll check the parking lot to
see if he's here. I know. If the truck isn't here I'll call the highway
patrol and the sheriff's office, have them start looking for him.
Now, what kind of truck was he driving? Truck number? All right,
Mrs. Collier, I'll call you back as soon as I know anything. Please
try not to worry too much."

Katie hung up the phone and looked at Rob. "I've got to take care of this. I just hope to god he's here."

"Katie, I heard you say Mrs. Collier. Was that Dan Collier's wife, Edie? From Longview, Texas?"

Katie looked at him in surprise. "Yes, but how did you?"

"Don't look so surprised," he said, smiling. "When you're in this business for a long time you get to know a lot of people. Dan used to drive for me when I had my trucks. Must be in his seventies by now. He's a good driver, hell of a nice guy. I want in, want to help in any way I can, okay?"

"Okay," Katie said.

Katie called security and they all went out in the storm, checked every row, every semi. Dan Collier's truck was not safely nestled in a space at Ghost Town.

"Want me to call her?" Rob asked when they got back to her office. "I know her pretty well."

"That would probably help," Katie said, "for her to be able to talk to somebody she knows."

Rob took the number from Katie and dialed the phone.

"Edie? This is Rob Townsend. Yes, sure has been. Listen, I'm here at Ghost Town and I heard about Dan. No, no Edie, he's not here. The highway patrol and sheriff's office have some people out looking for him. If they don't find him I'm going out first thing in the morning. I don't know. I'll get a snowmobile from somebody. We'll find him. Try not to worry. Dan's a pro. He's sure to have plenty of food and water. He's going to be all right. You just take care of yourself. I'll try to take care of things here. All right, you too. Goodnight now."

"You really think he's okay?" Katie asked.

"I want to think he is," Rob said. "If he didn't wreck it, he's got a good chance. It's only been two days."

"What about the cold? It's so cold, Rob."

"If he can't keep the engine running he's sure to have a candle and a coffee can. If you put that in a bunk and close all the curtains it'll keep you alive. Not warm, but alive. Now in case they don't find him tonight do you know where I can get my hands on a snowmobile?"

"My dad has one over at the house. He and Mom are out of town, they always head for Tucson in January, but I've got a key. If you have to go out tomorrow we can go over and get it."

She went over to him and put her arms around him. "I'm scared. I hope they find him tonight. I hope you don't have to go out tomorrow. I don't want anything to happen to you. It's so damn dangerous in the mountains when it snows like this."

"Don't go borrowing trouble, Ms. O'Connor. Especially not tomorrow's trouble. Never does any good you know." He kissed the top of her head. "Now how about a cup of coffee for a tired cowboy?"

CHAPTER EIGHT

When Katie walked into the dining room with Rob, Brad caught her attention and waved them over. "You find that guy's truck?" he asked.

"No, he didn't make it in. The sheriff's boys are out now. If they don't find him I'm going out in the morning," Rob said.

Brad looked at Rob. "I'd like to go along and help if I can. I was stranded once and I was sure glad people kept looking for me. Here, sit down, have dinner with us."

"Well," Rob said, "I sure would appreciate some help. If you really want to go I think we should try to be ready to leave by eight. How far is it to your folks' house, Katie?"

"Only about two miles. If we leave here at seven we should make it okay. I just wish...you guys be careful out there, okay? I'll have the kitchen pack lots of coffee and sandwiches and..."

"And we'll dress warm, Mother," Brad said, teasingly.

"Okay, okay, I'll quit worrying," Katie said, smiling at him. Katie jumped as she felt two little hands cover her eyes. "Jennifer!! You scared the shit out of me. Sit down, honey. We were just talking about trying to find that trucker who's missing."

"Yeah, I know." She glanced up at Rob and Brad. "I sure hope you find him. This storm is really bad." She turned to Katie. "I've been worrying about Jeremy. Has anybody checked on him lately?"

"Rob and I were up there yesterday. He was doing fine."

"Oh good, but do you think we could still go up there again? Tomorrow? Please? I really want to tell him about school."

Katie hesitated, thinking about the untouched pile of papers on her desk. "Sure," she said. "I'll pick you up after these two get going." She turned to Sandy. "Would you like to go? Might beat sitting around all day. We'll take along some food, make a party out of it."

Sandy smiled her slow, soft smile. "I'd like that," she said. "That'll help me not to worry."

"Worry?" Brad said. "Nothing to worry about. Two professional drivers here. By the way," he said to Rob, "how long have you been on the road?"

Rob laughed. "Too damn long," he said. "So long that it's hard for me to remember anything else. I used to rodeo when I was just a kid but I had to give that up when I busted my knee. Been driving trucks ever since."

"What'd you say your name was?" Brad asked.

"Rob Townsend."

"Yeah, yeah I thought I knew you from someplace. Rob? Rob Townsend? You rode bareback, a few bulls, roped a little too. You almost made rookie of the year when you cracked up. You don't remember me huh? Cherokee Kid?"

"I'll be damned. You really are? You're the Cherokee Kid? Shit, man, I remember you. The way you used to bulldog those steers. You were on my tail all year." Rob grinned. "You were a hell of a lot skinnier then."

Brad proudly patted his protruding belly.

The two men looked at each other with new respect. "How long have you been on the road?" Rob asked.

"Only about six years. Everything was downhill after I quit the rodeos. Nothing clicked for me and I mean nothing. I got myself a small ranch with my prize money, lost it. Lost a wife and a boy. The only good thing that happened to me was Sandy. Now we drive around, see the sights, take a couple of months off in the winter. It's okay. When I got my first driving job I took a truck to Boston. It was a flatbed and I'd never tarped a load before, never been east. I pulled over out of the way to put my tarps on, climbed up on the load, looked down on the other side, shit! I was on a bridge thing. It was at least five hundred feet down. I went flat, instant spider, inched my way off that load."

"Earn while you learn time," Rob said, laughing.

"Still learning," Brad said.

"Why do you guys do it?" Katie asked. "It has to be a hard way to make a living."

"It sure is," Brad said. "Buddy of mine says that trucking is an honest way to make a hard living. There's truth in that."

"Sure is," Rob said.

"You know, a long time ago, when my boy was with me, I really used to love it. It was, I don't know." Rob stopped, grinned. "I used to tell him it was all a game. See if you could outsmart em, the scales, cops, DOT. Trucking, the playin' of the game. Now? I don't even know if I like it. Still, some things, like you have this illusion of freedom. You're not really free but you feel free. And it's a challenge even now, after all these years. It measures a person, stretches you, mentally and physically. You feel a little like a different breed, set apart somehow. Like sometimes late at night, you've about had it and another big one passes you. You dim your lights to let him know he can get back in and he flashes his running lights to say 'Thanks, buddy.' You perk up a little, feel less alone." Rob's voice trailed off.

"I think it's an escape, the great escape," Sandy said softly.

"Escape?" Katie wondered.

Sandy nodded. "Yes, escape. It's so hard, so demanding, all your energy, everything in you is taken up by the job. It's so real, so, so awful, everything else fades into the background. Heck of an escape, huh?" She laughed, stopped abruptly, covering her mouth with her hand, as if she was surprised at herself for saying so much.

Brad looked at her proudly. "I'm glad Sandy is with me. That makes it okay. But even then it's a different life, a hard life. Like you said, you feel like a different breed, call non truckers civilians. I don't take it too seriously though," he said, grinning. "I like to bullshit. Maybe that's why I like it. Truckers are all bullshitters."

"Yep," Rob said, laughing. "That's probably about the best thing you can say about the trucking industry. It's full of bullshitters. Hell of a note isn't it?"

They had all finished dinner and were about ready to leave when Jennifer noticed the four girls and their pimp. They were all laughing, shaking snow out of their hair, as they came into the dining room.

"Well, what have we here," Brad said whistling low.

The girls looked young, young girls, old faces, all wearing high heels, skin tight dresses, net stockings, and thick mascara. The mascara seemed to emphasize the deep emptiness in their eyes, eyes that were too empty, too old, for their young/old faces. He had on a rich brown suit and a silk shirt. A soft brown fedora was pulled low over one of his eyes. His eyes were not old, his face not young.

Jennifer watched, watched as he smiled at his girls, leaned back expansively in his chair. *Bet he buys them a good dinner tonight. Snow storms are good for his kind of business, his kind of shit.*

"Wonder where they've been holed up?" Brad asked.

"Probably at the motel, just off the exit," Katie said.

Everyone in the restaurant was watching them. Some of the watchers were amused, some embarrassed.

Jennifer was not amused. She did not feel embarrassed. Jennifer felt ashamed. Her cheeks felt hot. Why were they here? Were they her, a part of her? Was she just like them?

CHAPTER NINE

Rob walked her out to the jeep.
He put his hand on her shoulder. "Spend the night with me, Katie."

She shook her head no, got in the jeep and headed out of the parking lot.

What in the hell are you doing? The last thing in the world you want to do is go home, sleep alone.

I'm scared. I'm scared he'll leave. I can't handle this. It's all too fast. I don't know him. Not really.

Don't borrow trouble, especially not tomorrow's trouble. Isn't that what he said, what you're doing? What about right now? Tonight? What do you want to do with this night, this time ?

I want Rob to hold me, love me.

Katie turned the jeep around.

CHAPTER TEN

Katie knocked timidly on his door.
No one answered.

She knocked again, louder. "Rob?"

He came to the door, saw her standing in the snow. He half lifted her into the truck, pulling her into his arms. "You okay with this?" he asked.

"Yes, yes I am," she said.

Strong gentle hands
cupped her face

Finger tips
tracing

Eyes
Lips
Cheeks

Hands touching
holding

Firm high breasts
nipples erect

Soft warm
flesh

Soft sigh
of opening thighs

Sharp intake of breath

"My god I…I…"

Mouth, lips, tongue

Hot pulsing center

Sweet unbearable warmth

They lay tangled together. The bunk was warm, smelled of sweat and sex. Good smells.

Katie looked down at Rob. He looked so young, peaceful, so beautiful in sleep. She felt protective, at the same time protected.

Katie reached out shyly, tracing his eyebrows with her fingertips. She touched his lips with hers, lightly, so lightly. He smiled, a soft smile. "Don't stop now," he said.

She moved her hand, tracing a line from his chin to his belly button, too shy to do more. Rob took her hand, moved it lower.

Katie snuggled down in his arms, holding him warmly in her hand.

THURSDAY
January 16, 1985

CHAPTER ONE

Dan woke up slowly out of an uneasy sleep. He switched on the dome light and checked his watch. 3:40 in the morning? The afternoon? He was hungry for some good hot food, for bacon and eggs and a pot of fresh coffee. He was cold too, not freezing to death, but cold and weak and cramped and starting to smell and...

I'm scared, Edie. Really scared.

Better get em out, honey, get those guys looking for me.

Edie. He could see her in his head, plain as day. She was a short, ample woman with short, curly, grey hair. She was a lady, his lady. She'd be with him now if she hadn't had a bad cold when he took off on this run. *Glad she's safe. Glad she's not here. Nope. Don't do that, old man. Don't get maudlin on me. Don't start writing any farewell letters, not even in your head. Not necessary. Not now. Not yet.*

Dan looked at his remaining food supplies, made a wry face.

What'll you have tonight, mister?

How 'bout some biscuits and gravy?

Sorry, we're all out a biscuits.

Well then, can I just have the gravy? Piping hot. Hot coffee.

Sorry. We're all out of gravy.
Coffee.

Well, what in the hell do you
have for a hungry man to eat?

Spaghetti and meat balls, sir. But,
uh, our stove is on the blink so
you'll have to eat em cold.

Well, that's the way it'll have to
be I guess. Remind me to never,
ever stop at this damn truck stop
again.

Dan opened the can of spaghetti and meat balls and started to
eat the damn stuff.

CHAPTER TWO

"**K**atie?"

"Mmm?"

"You awake?"

She laughed, a deep, throaty, sexy woman laugh.

"Am now."

Just before dawn, Rob stuck his head out of the bunk. He got up and went to the window.

"My god, it's finally stopped. Katie, the snow stopped."

Katie sat up, pulling the covers around her, feeling suddenly cold. "Rob, it's not time yet is it, it's not daylight yet."

He sat back down beside her and kissed her lightly. "Ssshhh." Rob cupped her face in his hands and kissed her eyes, the tip of her nose. He lay down beside her, holding her close.

CHAPTER THREE

Katie watched them until they were out of sight. She wandered through her parents' house, went to the room that used to he hers. She ran her hands lightly over the dresser, knelt down by the bed.

Dear, God. Please keep them safe. Please let them find Mr. Collier and let him be okay and, and thank you for Rob. Amen.

Katie got up, gave one last look around her room, her childhood home and went to see if Jennifer wanted a ride to Ghost Town.

"Jennifer?"

Katie knocked on Jennifer's door again, tried the knob.

"Jennifer?"

She was sitting on her workbench, slender body bent over, shaking with sobs.

Katie crossed the room and took her in her arms. "It's okay, honey. It's okay," she said stroking the girl's hair.

Jennifer cried for a long time. When the sobs finally stopped Katie went into the bathroom and got a warm washcloth and towel. She washed Jennifer's face and gently patted it dry. She sat down, took Jennifer's hands in hers. "Want to talk about it?" she asked.

"I don't know, Katie. I don't know what's wrong with me, why I feel so awful, so empty." She gulped, fighting back new tears.

"No, no that's not true. I don't feel empty. I feel dirty. Like I'll never ever be clean, be free of it. I was so happy about school," she stopped, rubbed her fists against her eyes, five years old going on eighteen. "Then I think, how could anybody want me in their school? I'm not, I'm just, all those men. Sometimes they gave me money, presents. And I think, shit. Just because I'm going to school that won't change who I am, how awful I am. Last night, when those girls walked in with their pimp, remember?"

"Yes, I remember," Katie said slowly.

"Everybody either laughed, or said something, or looked away embarrassed. Everybody except me. I felt, I felt like, well here they are, all dressed up. Is that me? Am I just like them, just not a professional? Am I? Oh God, I just don't know. There have been so many men, I feel like shit, like a dirty little shit."

Katie waited until the new tears stopped.

"Jennifer! Look at me, damn it!"

Jennifer looked up.

"You're a beautiful, beautiful person, honey. You. You're kind and sensitive and talented. Most people would give anything to have the kind of talent you have." Katie took her face in her hands. "You're a beautiful, worthwhile person and you aren't dirty.

"Honey, there are perfectly good reasons why you, why you've been with different men. When I was a teacher I took some classes about sexual abuse. I learned about what happens to kids who have gone through the kind of hell you went through. Girls who have gone through that kind of horror sometimes do sleep with lots of different men. Think about it, honey. That's how you were taught to relate to men, taught by the most significant man in your young life. Richard did this, Jennifer, he taught you to relate to men that way."

"Yeah, Richard taught me. He taught me so many things. He taught me to hate," Jennifer said bitterly. "He taught me to be afraid. He taught me to brush my teeth and wash my face. He taught me to suck his dick," she said, her voice hard, angry. "He taught me," bitter laugh, "everything I know."

Jennifer looked squarely at Katie. "And then he paid me. He gave me presents, took me on trips, gave me money. Lots of money. And I took it. And I hate him, I hate that god damn fucking bastard. I hate him, I hate him, I..." fists pounding on the work bench. She crumpled up, crying again. "But, Katie, some part of me loved him, still loved him, wanted it to be true. What people thought. That he was my daddy. That we were a family. That I was...and then I think it must be me, my fault. Must have had WHORE written right across my forehead or he wouldn't have treated me like one. WHORE. Me. Little Jennifer."

Katie pulled her close, cradled her in her arms. "No five year old child has whore written across her forehead," she said firmly. "No little girl is to blame when some man abuses her. You were a baby, a little girl. You weren't dirty or bad or sick. What happened was not your fault, not in any way. Richard is the sick person, not you.

"What's important is now, honey. Today. Tomorrow. There are people who can help you understand what happened to you, help you learn to deal with it. When we go to New York we'll find those people. So you can understand, so it doesn't control the rest of your life. If you let it control you then Richard has won and I don't want that sick bastard to win anything."

Jennifer looked up, surprised at the anger in Katie's voice.

"Okay?" Katie asked. "Deal?"

"Deal," Jennifer said. "Aunt Katie?"

Katie felt her own eyes fill with tears. Jennifer hadn't called her Aunt Katie in years, not since she was a very little girl. "Yes, honey?"

"I love you," Jennifer said softly, looking the other way.

Katie hugged her close. "I love you too," she said. "Very, very much."

CHAPTER FOUR

The snowmobile glided easily along on top of the snow, passing up the big snow plows that were straining against the drifts, searching for the interstate. It was an unbelievably beautiful day. The air was still bitter cold, but there was no wind, and that big Montana sky was blue and sunny. Rob felt a guilty sense of exhilaration. It felt so damn good to be alive, to be out in all of this. They traveled forty miles north, fifty, eyes intent, but they saw nothing.

Brad brought the noisy machine to a stop. "What about it? Think we should go any farther?"

Rob shook his head. "From what Edie said he would have gotten at least this far. Somewhere behind us, between here and Ghost Town, Dan Collier and that semi are buried. We've just missed it."

"Yeah," Brad said. "Unless he went off the road and wrecked it. Then we won't find him till spring."

"I know," Rob said, "but let's keep after it. Take it real slow going back, keep looking, for anything. Damn it, I think he's here. I think he's alive."

"Okay," Brad said, turning the snowmobile around.

They were only about fifteen miles from Ghost Town when Rob saw it, a small, very small, puff of smoke. He let out a yell, a whoop of laughter.

Brad stopped the snowmobile, skidding around sharply. Rob pointed toward the smoke. "He's there, in there. See the smoke?" He pounded Brad on the back.

"What the, where?" Brad asked, still not seeing anything. "You're going snow blind, man. Ain't nothing there."

Rob didn't answer him. He was already headed toward the side of the road carrying one of the shovels. "Just be alive when we get in there, old buddy." he said.

Dan Collier was fast asleep when they finally broke through the snow and got the door of his semi open. Rob and Brad stood there at the open door, looking at each other. "Want me to go in?" Brad asked.

"No, that's okay. Thanks but I'll check," Rob said. "Maybe you better get on the CB, get some medics out here."

Rob climbed up in the cab and pulled back the curtains that led to the bunk. Dan was lying there, lying so quietly that for a minute Rob thought they were too late. He reached out tentatively, touched his old friend on the shoulder.

"Dan? Dan! Wake up, buddy, wake up," Rob said, gently shaking him.

Dan started to come around then. He sat up, blinking his eyes in the too bright light, looking around, confused and disoriented. "Rob? Rob Townsend? What the, am I still asleep? I, I've been buried here the longest..." He started to cry, tears running down his face. "Oh God, I've been so scared." Arms trembling, reaching for Rob.

Rob hugged him close, patting him awkwardly on the back, tears in his own eyes.

"Well," Rob said, "what do you say we get the hell out of here, get you checked out by some of those fancy medical experts."

He stood up and gently lifted the slight old man out of the bunk. He carried him to the open door, carried him back to fresh air and sunshine and the far away sound of help headed their way.

CHAPTER FIVE

Randy checked himself in the mirror. His face was still pale and he had stitches over his right eye and some more on the top of his head. He was all dressed up in a navy blue suit, white shirt, tie, all dressed up for Jimmy's funeral.

It was almost time to go. Randy wandered into the living room. Teddy was sprawled on the sofa, headphones on, oblivious to everything and everybody. Randy touched him on the shoulder. Teddy looked up, took the headphones off. "Time to go, Teddy," Randy said.

Teddy shook his head. "I'm not going, man, can't go," he said, putting the headphones back on.

"Okay," Randy said.

The wealthy seem to do everything well, even funerals, Randy thought as he looked around the church. Understated elegance, understated grief. Intelligent, emotionless religion. Intelligent, emotionless funeral. The minister spoke eloquently, intelligently, about James Lynn Baxter and his brief but nevertheless meaningful and full life.

Randy couldn't find anything of his friend or his friend's life in that church, among those people.

Randy wanted to tell them about the real Jimmy.

The Jimmy who befriended a lonely young Texan. The Jimmy

who could laugh, really laugh, deep belly laughs. The Jimmy who stayed up all night with Teddy when he was on a bad trip. About his mind, the incredible way he could get off on philosophy. About the way he would get this puzzled, wistful look, wanting to find something, some truth.

It was over, done with. Jimmy wasn't here, hadn't been here.

Randy walked out of the church, hands stuffed deep in his pockets, wondering why in the hell the best friend he had ever had in the whole world had to be lying in a god damn flower covered casket when the god damn fucking sun was shining and the light snow that was falling was so damn beautiful it made him hurt all over. Made him want to cry.

CHAPTER SIX

The car rolled along the dirt road that led to Old Old Grandma's house, windows rolled tight against the billowing clouds of dust, air conditioner trying in vain to fight the hot Texas summer sun.

Seven year old Randy looked out the window. He knew the way to Old Old Grandma's house almost by heart but today's trip was different. Today they had come to say goodbye. That's what his dad had told him, that it was time to say goodbye.

"Why'd she die, Dad?" Randy had asked

"Well, she was very old. Ninety-seven. I think she just got tired, you know, was just ready to rest."

"Was she sick?"

"No, no not really. Just kind of tired and worn out and ready to let go. You remember, the last few times we went to see her, remember where she always wanted us to take her?"

Randy shook his head no.

"To the cemetery. Remember? And she'd show you where my grandpa was buried, her two children, and then she'd say, 'And this is my place, this is where I'll lay one day, Randy.'"

"Yeah," Randy said, smiling, "and then we'd go back to her house and have beans and cornbread and apple pie and...I wish, I wish she wasn't dead."

"I do too, Randy, but you know, she had a good, long life. She saw her kids, grandkids, all grown. Saw you. She was sure crazy about you, only great grandson she ever had. Course if she'd had twenty she would have still been crazy about you," Rob said, messing up the boy's hair.

When they got to the cemetery, and the minister had finished with his prayers, he asked Randy to place the symbolic first shovel of earth in the grave. "You are her future, son," he said gently.

Old Old Grandma was gone.

They went back to the church and there were tables full of food. There were aunts and uncles and cousins, and everywhere the memories.

> She was some cook. Say that. Always made her beans with rain water. Said that was the secret.
>
> Washed her hair in rain water too. Said it kept it soft, young. Sure had beautiful hair.
>
> Spitfire. Why I remember she kicked old George out one night…
>
> Never missed a Sunday at church, even when she was sick.
>
> We were girls together, used to sit under that big oak down by the old school, cut out paper dolls, make dresses for them. Made dolls out of hollyhocks, beautiful hollyhock dolls. Do little girls still do that today? …creaky, trembling voice.

Randy watched and listened and stored it all up inside. *I am her future*, he thought, not exactly sure what that meant, but feeling very, very proud.

CHAPTER SEVEN

It had been a good day, a bright, shiny penny kind of day. Jeremy had fixed a big kettle of stew and with the food Katie had brought along they had a veritable feast for lunch. Jeremy and Sandy had taken an instant liking to each other, an innocent to innocent, child to child, liking.

Jennifer had been sad and distant earlier in the day but she started sketching after lunch and the shadows all lifted. She was curled up by the fireplace, slender body bent gracefully forward, long blonde hair falling softly around her face. Katie felt a familiar pang as she watched her.

Why, why in the hell didn't I know? How could I not have known? All the signs were there. And when I used to visit, the hand she would slip in mine would cling so tightly.

And Peg, lying there dead. Booze and pills, he said, and we all just accepted it. He was her husband. Her doctor.

And we walked away and left Jennifer there with him and she was so quiet, so well behaved. And he so damn attentive, so loving.

Why didn't I try harder to convince
her to come with us? After the
funeral I should have brought her
home, I...

Katie went over to her. "Can I see what you've done?"

Jennifer showed Katie the two sketches she had made, two different views of Jeremy and Sandy.

"They're wonderful, honey," Katie said.

"Yeah, but I should have brought some charcoal. You know. For contours, shadows." She got up, went to the fireplace, scooped up some cold ashes. "These might work," she said, spreading the ashes deftly, expertly, giving depth, shadows to the faces on the sketch pad.

"There. Now I'm satisfied. Well almost satisfied," Jennifer said smiling. She got up and gave one picture to Jeremy, one to Sandy.

"That's so, that's me, me and Jeremy. Thank you, thank you so much," Sandy said, hugging Jennifer.

"You're welcome," Jennifer said.

"I think I'll make a frame," Jeremy said. "A red, white, and blue frame."

CHAPTER EIGHT

Katie had dropped Jennifer off at her apartment and was driving Sandy back to Ghost Town. Sandy kept looking at her. "You're different today. Softer." She laughed. "Rob, huh? You're in love. Glowing."

Katie grinned. "Is it that obvious?"

"Sure is," Sandy said. "You're happy, huh?"

"Yes, but it, it scares me a little," Katie said. "I haven't cared about anybody, wanted anybody, for a long time. So I'm happy, but I'm also scared. Scared he'll leave. Scared that even if he doesn't, if he stays, if things work out, what then? He's a trucker and he'll be gone all the time and...boy, talk about jumping ahead of myself," Katie said, laughing. "I've only known him for a little while."

"Sometimes it doesn't take long, knew Brad for three weeks, he wouldn't go away," she said, laughing, "So I finally went with him. We've been married twelve years now. So don't worry so much. Besides, if it all works out you could always go with him, on the road."

"I guess I could. But then I hear all of you talking, I don't know if I could handle living like that."

"You handle it or you handle living alone," Sandy said. "It's not easy, either way. I always have to make hard choices, be with Brad, or stay home with our son Larry. It's hard both ways but I mostly like being on the road, like driving. Besides I just, I don't sleep good without Brad."

"I don't know," Katie said. "No showers, no sleep. Dirty restrooms. I don't know how you do it. I feel like such a wimp sometimes."

"I don't think you're a wimp," Sandy said, giggling. "Run Ghost Town pretty good. It must take a pretty tough lady to do that. It's the best truck stop around. You can be really proud of that."

Katie smiled. "Thanks, thanks for saying that."

"Is Jennifer okay?" Sandy asked then. "She seemed so quiet."

Katie looked over at Sandy. "I don't know. I hope she'll be okay. She's so down on herself, so sad. She was, her stepdad really messed her up when she was a little kid. I feel so awful about it, so guilty about not knowing what was going on."

"Don't be too hard on yourself," Sandy said. "It's hard for people to believe things like that happen. Happens a lot I think." She hesitated. "Happened to me once," she said softly. "He was some uncle or cousin or something. I was so little I don't really know. I don't remember much about it. Remember the quiet. The way he smelled, all sour and sweaty with fat, dirty fingers. Remember my mama, remember her eyes and the big knife that came out of her skirt.

"I have it now," Sandy said, more softly still. "The big knife. Have it with me always."

Katie looked at her, startled. "You? You have a knife?" Katie laughed, laughed so hard tears rolled down her cheeks. "You're so soft and quiet. Shy. And all this time..."

Sandy sat there demurely, hands folded in her lap, laughter behind her soft brown eyes.

"Sandy?"

"Yes?"

"I'm glad your mother had that knife, glad you have it now. I wish, I wish my sister would have saved Jennifer the way your mother saved you."

CHAPTER NINE

Everybody at Ghost Town was caught up in the excitement. A trucker had been saved and every driver there felt relieved, happy, knowing that it could have easily been one of them who had been buried under that mountain of snow.

They kept stopping by to talk to Rob and Brad, congratulating them, pounding them on the back, asking questions, wanting to hear the story over and over again.

How'd you know he was in there, man?

No kidding, did you think he was dead when he didn't come to the door?

No shit? He's really in his seventies? Is he okay? What'd the doc say?

How'd the interstate look? Hear they're going to open it sometime soon.

What really happened? Snow slide? Remind me to be careful where I pull over in these damn mountains.

They were all so happy. Jennifer was glad that Mr. Collier was okay, glad that everybody was safe, but she felt so isolated, alone, even though she was sitting between Katie and Sandy she felt terribly, terribly alone. Cold.

Katie turned to her. "You okay, honey?" she asked, concern in her voice.

"Sure," Jennifer said. "Sure, I'm okay." She got up, gave Katie a hug, and headed for the restroom. "I need to get ready for work. Ben said he wanted to spend some time with me tonight. I think he's already missing me," Jennifer smiled, a smile that seemed to chase some of the shadows away.

"Tell Ben hi for me, honey, and be careful, it's really, really cold out there."

"Yes, Mother," Jennifer said, giving Katie another hug.

Jennifer opened the restroom door and there they were. They were in there, two of them, in her restroom. The other two were probably outside, knocking on doors, turning tricks, collecting money.

Jennifer waited until they left. She studied her face in the mirror and ran a comb through her hair. Jennifer went to the gift shop, knowing that soon Ben would come through that door, hold her close, keep her safe, keep her away from other truckers, other trucks.

CHAPTER TEN

The crowd in the dining room had finally thinned out. Brad and Sandy had left, gone to bed. Rob tipped his chair back, hands behind his head, grinned at her. "Your place or mine, ma'am?" he asked.

Katie shook her head, laughing. "Pretty sure of yourself, aren't you?" she asked.

"Yep."

"Let's go up the hill. I haven't been home for a while," she said, smiling.

The little house was warm and comfortable. Rob looked around. "It's like you, Katie," he said, taking her in his arms. "It's beautiful and warm and honest. I like it very much."

They were sitting in front of the fire, content, toes touching.

"Rob?"

"Mmm?"

"Do you think we might be, that we're…"

"Falling in love?" he finished.

She nodded.

He reached out, touched her cheek. "Very possible," he said. "Still scared?"

"Yes," she said softly, "yes I am. Are you? Scared?"

He thought about it for a while. "S'pose so," he said slowly. "I think any time you have something happen, a divorce, a death, it's scary to think about trying again, scary to care enough to risk getting hurt again."

"Did you love her?" Katie asked, her voice small.

Rob lit a cigarette, sat staring into the fire.

"Did you? Love her?"

He looked at her. "Yes, yes I loved her. In the beginning it was good between us."

"What happened?"

He shrugged. "Whatever happens? For a while we were walking along down the same path, arm in arm, laughing. Then all of a sudden, or it seemed all of a sudden, that big old straight path ended, split off into two little trails. She took one path, I took the other. Not necessarily bad but, see, neither one of us, we didn't try, just didn't ever share our lives, our different paths with each other.

"You know," he said, staring into the fire again. "When you look at someone through the eyes of love you see one picture. When you look at that same person through the eyes of bitterness, resentment, you see a totally different picture, react to that person in a different way. I guess we just forgot to look at each other through the eyes of love."

"You've thought about it a lot," Katie said softly.

"Yeah, yeah I have. Trucking gives you that. Lots of thinking time."

"Do you miss her?"

"I did. Not now. Not for a long time. Still miss my boy though. Miss him a lot."

He smiled at her, reached out, messed up her hair. "And no, no I don't still love her, okay?"

"Okay," Katie said, smiling back at him.

CHAPTER ELEVEN

Abraham had started his day with cold coffee and a couple of white crosses. He had been drinking coffee all day, popping an occasional cross whenever he felt himself getting low.

Sleep had eluded him for two nights now. It was almost eleven o'clock and still his eyes were wide open, his head pounding.

Abraham wanted to get the hell out of there. He climbed out of the bunk and switched on his radio, checking out the road situation. Same old story. The interstate was still closed. Maybe it would open in the morning.

Abraham turned off his light, switched off the radio and leaned back in his seat. He looked around the parking lot. The dome light came on in a big black Eagle about six trucks down and Abraham saw Jennifer climbing out of the bunk. She sat down in the passenger's seat and combed her tousled, blonde hair. A man joined her, running his fingers through his long. reddish hair.

Little whore, Abraham thought, *dirty little whore*. He watched as they sat there talking, feeling the anger build.

Thought she was a good little girl, going away to school, just another whore with a little girl's face, just like my fine mama.

"I won't be back through until next Thursday, Jenny. You'll still be here, right?"

Jennifer smiled at him, brushed back the hair that was hanging over his forehead. "Yes, I'll still be here. I'm not really sure about the timeline, Ben, but...I, I don't want to lose you just because I'm leaving, going to school. I'm not very good at saying, not good at telling people how I feel. You're very...oh shit."

"Honey, it's okay. I'm just scared you won't be interested in a trucker once you go to New York. I've told you before, I love you and I don't want to lose you."

Jennifer hugged him close, rested her head on his chest, breathed in the safe, real smells of the gentle young man. "I'm going to get out of here now, let you get some sleep. The interstate is supposed to open in the morning and I want you to get some rest before you head for Los Angeles."

Jennifer jumped lightly down from the truck.

"Hey, wait just a minute." Ben climbed out of the truck, shivering in his wool shirt. "I'm walking you back to your car."

Jennifer gave him a little shove, laughed. "Don't be a dork, Ghost Town is still open. You get back in that truck and get some sleep." She gave Ben another hug and walked off down the long row of trucks.

Jennifer was halfway back to the truck stop when she stopped, listening. She stood there undecided, alone in the dark. Was someone following her?

Jennifer heard his footsteps, his heavy breathing. Someone was coming after her, in the deep snow, in the dark. Jennifer started to run, her heart's wings beating frantically under her soft breasts. She ran until she was out of breath, slid under an empty trailer, lay there quietly, trembling.

He was coming. He was going to find her. Find her. Hurt her. He was going to hurt her, like he always hurt her. Hurt her so badly. He...

Little Jennifer is hiding
under her bed.

She stuffs her fist in her mouth.

Lies there quietly.

Cruel hands reach for her.

Pull her out.

"Mommie!" she cries.

"Quiet!"

Little Jennifer is quiet.

The footsteps stopped. Abraham reached under the trailer and pulled her out. Muffled sobs.

"Quiet!"

Jennifer was quiet. His hands twisted cruelly in her hair. "Whore," he said. "Nothing but a whore. Look so fine. So pure. Fucking whore. Whore, whore, whore." Rhythmically, rhythmically banging her head against the heavy metal trailer. The hands pulled out of her hair, hung limp at his side, limp as she was limp, lying still in the deep, soft snow, long blonde hair matted with blood, small child's face white, white as the snow was white.

Abraham leaned heavily against the trailer. He was trembling, filled with fear and renewed anger. Why? Why did she have to come? Why did she have to be so wicked, such a wicked, wanton whore? It was her fault, all her fault.

It was still there, still pounding, pounding in his head, his temples, behind his eyes. Pounding. Dark, insistent anger. *Let me out...let me out*! screamed the dark angry beast.

His heavy steel tipped boots kicked out savagely, and still the beast was trapped, pounding, demanding release.

His hands fumbled with her clothes, sweat rolling down his face in the bitter night air. Abraham shook her. "Wake up. Wake up, Whore. Wake up…"

The knife, shiny, erect, forged with strength. HIS instrument, the instrument of the Lord. The light of the Lord.

"Which one shall I put in you, whore. Which one?" He grabbed her by the hair. Shook her. "Answer me, whore. Why don't you answer me? Look at me, whore. Tell me what you want."

Jennifer couldn't hear. Jennifer couldn't feel. It was too dark to see, too dark to feel.

Then black, red pain broke through the blessed darkness. "Mommie! Mommieee, he's hurting me, Mommieeeee…"

FRIDAY
January 17, 1985

CHAPTER ONE

Jeremy wanted to go to Ghost Town. It had already been too long, too many days, nights, confined. The snow had stopped and the plows had been out. There were tracks. He was brave and strong, he could make it.

It was still dark outside. Pre-dawn, the quiet time, the sleeping time, Jeremy's time. He set out slowly, fat puppy tumbling along behind him.

It was as he knew it would be, pre-dawn, sleeping monsters. He walked quietly up and down the rows, marveling at the size of the big trucks. His long overcoat flapped around his knees as he made his way slowly around his circle.

He was almost done, almost ready to leave Ghost Town, when he heard the puppy whining behind him. He turned and saw the puppy sitting next to an empty trailer, next to a small, quiet, little girl.

Jeremy walked slowly over to her.

"Poor little girl," he said, kneeling down beside her. "Poor little Jennifer. You got to get up. You're going to school."

He picked up the shiny, steel blade and quickly laid it down again.

"Poor little girl. You're cold, huh?"

Jeremy took off his old overcoat and laid it gently over Jennifer. He tucked it in around her and sat beside her, holding her still, cold hand in his.

CHAPTER TWO

The green and white freightliner eased quietly, slowly, out of the parking lot.

Abraham had waited, forced himself to wait, sat there trembling, sweat soaking through his heavy work shirt, his coveralls, running down his body. It was safe now, safe to leave. Three, four, five trucks had already pulled out and headed south. His would not be the first. His would not be the only one. His would be one among many.

Many trucks. Many miles.

Safety.

So many trucks. Nothing, absolutely nothing to connect him to the still, white girl child with the frozen red blood flowing between her legs.

The pounding in his head had stopped, quieted. The beast was asleep, sated, cleansed, cleansed in the blood, the blood of the lamb. Such a small lamb, so small, a girl child. A damsel, crying, but no one heard. No one came. No one had come to stop the angry, pounding beast.

> "For he found her in the field, and
> the damsel cried, and there was
> none to save her."

"None to save her," he said again, wonderingly. "Why, why didn't somebody save her?" he asked then, starting to cry.

CHAPTER THREE

It was one thing to wake up at home and have to pee but it was quite another to wake up in the back of a damn truck with a bladder so full it hurt, and the truck stop restrooms far away down a long row of sleeping trucks.

"Damn," Sandy said. She pulled on a pair of coveralls and some old boots, kissed her sleeping husband on the cheek, and headed across the parking lot.

She was trudging through the deep snow, gritting her teeth, when she saw them, saw them in the still shadowy, indistinct light but, "Oh my God, no, not this, not Jennifer, not, oh my God."

Sandy turned and ran back to the truck, long braid flying behind her. "Brad! Brad, wake up! Come help!" She grabbed some blankets from the bunk and pounded on Brad's shoulder. "Brad, wake up! Damn it! Come help me." Sandy ran out, pulling the blankets behind her.

Brad sat up, rubbing his shoulder, trying to figure out what in the hell was going on. *Sandy pounded on me. What'd she do that for?* he wondered.

When he got there, he saw Sandy wrapping blankets around some old guy, trying to help him, get him up. Geez, the old guy looked half dead, ice even on his eyelashes. From tears?

"Oh shit," Brad said, seeing Jennifer lying there under the long old coat. "Oh shit," tears in his own eyes.

"Come on, old fellow, we'll get you inside, warmed up," Brad said. Jeremy's voice wasn't working too well but Brad understood. He scooped up the little puppy and they made their way across the parking lot.

CHAPTER FOUR

This can't be, isn't real. It's a bad dream. I'm going to wake up any minute now, wake up at home, get a cup of coffee, wake up, wake up, Katie O'Connor, damn it wake up...

"Ma'am?"

The young police sergeant cleared his throat. "I, we need someone to identify the victim. Does she have any family, anyone who can come?"

"I'm her family," Katie said. "She's my niece. I'm the only family she has. I'll go." Her voice sounded flat, emotionless.

They drove in silence to the place they had taken her, Katie and Rob, the young sergeant. The room was cold. The young sergeant pulled out a drawer and uncovered a face.

Everything inside of her wanted to come up, come out, wanted to splash all over the clean, cold, sterile floor, splash on the shiny, squeaky clean boots of the shiny, squeaky clean young sergeant. She fought it down.

"Yes. Yes that's Jennifer, Jennifer Davis. She's my niece. I'm the only family she has. I'll make all the funeral arrangements." Katie's calm, dead, emotionless voice echoed eerily in her head. Why am I just standing here, how can I sound so calm, reasonable, when Jennifer is, Oh God, Jennifer is, Oh God, dead, dead, like Joe, Little Joe, no, no, no, not now, not Jennifer, not...

She turned away, dry eyed. Rob put his arm around her shoulders. She looked up at him. "He'll not know, not be notified. He will *never* have her back, not even now, not ever."

When they got back from the morgue, Jeremy was still in her office, wrapped in Sandy's blankets. Katie walked over to Jeremy and put her arms around him. They stood that way until the young sergeant walked through the door.

"I need to take the old man in for questioning," he said, nodding at Jeremy.

Katie looked at the sergeant. "You aren't serious. You aren't taking him to jail. Not Jeremy. You're crazy. He couldn't hurt anybody. He was trying to help, to keep her warm."

"We need to ask him a few questions, ma'am. We have to try to find out what happened."

"Can't you question him here?" Katie pleaded. "You'll kill him if you take him to jail, kill him. He's been sitting out there in the cold for God knows how long. He needs to see a doctor. Please let me take him to a doctor. He can't stand to be caged in. Rob, please don't let them take him. He didn't do anything." Katie started to cry.

"I know, Katie, I know," Rob said, pulling her close.

The sergeant went over to Jeremy and snapped a pair of handcuffs around his wrists. Katie pulled away from Rob and ran across the room, grabbing the sergeant's arm.

"Don't, don't do that. Please," she said, fighting to remain calm, rational. "Please don't do that. He doesn't understand. Just let me drive him downtown, talk to him, stay with him. Let me try to explain, so he'll know it's not forever, so…"

The sergeant shook his head. "Sorry, ma'am."

She slapped him then, hard, slapped his unfeeling, shiny, squeaky clean face, started pounding on him with her fists.

Rob wrapped his arms around her and held her close, held her until she finally stopped struggling, until Jeremy was gone and they could no longer hear the siren wailing in the distance.

"Let me go, let me go, dammit, Rob, just let me go."

Katie paced across the room. *Twenty paces across, twenty paces back.*

Lisa was standing in the doorway, wide eyed, face white. Rob went over to her. "Lisa, call her doctor. Tell him we need him to come to her house. I'll drive her home." Rob put his hands on the young girl's shoulders and gently pushed her through the door.

Katie kept pacing. "They're killing him, killing him, Rob. He can't stand to be shut up. They can't do this, I've got to make them stop, got to go there, get him out. He's so scared of being trapped, so scared."

Rob put his arms around her. "Come on, Katie. I'm taking you home now. We'll get Jeremy out, I promise, I'll go there first thing in the morning."

He gently wrapped her coat around her and led her out to the jeep.

CHAPTER FIVE

Jeremy looked down at his wrists. He twisted his hands again, twisted them until they were raw and red blood stained the shiny, metal cuffs and still he was trapped.

He was in a cage. The cage was inside of a car. The cage had heavy wire and no doors and he knew he could not get out and there was a shrill terrible noise above his head and he wanted to go home.

Pretty soon the terrible noise stopped and the car stopped and the man opened a door in the cage and Jeremy was standing in a big garage and he couldn't see the sky and he couldn't smell the wind and he wanted to go home and feed the puppy and see if the squirrels and the winter birds had enough food. He wanted to walk up to the stream behind the cabin and see the icy blue water running swift under the ice. Running free.

They took him down a long hall to another cage and this cage was bigger but there were no windows and it seemed very dark, inside dark, the kind of dark that scared him. They took off the shiny metal cuffs and pushed him inside. Then they slid the big steel door shut.

CHAPTER SIX

R ob sat beside her bed. He wanted to be there when she woke up. He wanted to hold her, reassure her, tell her it was okay, that it was all over.

All over? Just beginning? How would she deal with all of this, with losing Jennifer, losing another child? And Jeremy. Poor old guy. Anybody with half a brain could see he couldn't, wouldn't, ever hurt anybody. He would go down there in the morning, see what could be done about bail, about getting the old guy out of there.

All over?

The police had come and gone. The TV cameras had come and gone. The newspaper reporters had come and gone. The doctor had come and gone.

Rob? Rob had come and stayed.

Katie stirred, crying out softly in her sleep. Rob leaned over, brushed the hair off of her face.

"I love you, Katie O' Connor," he said softly.

CHAPTER SEVEN

They had lived in the apartment for almost two years. Teddy, Jimmy and Randy. Three friends, high school buddies, college roommates. Three roommates, now there were two.

Teddy was sitting cross legged on the floor, booze and Maui Wowi profound. "Nothin's real, buddy. Nothing. All illusions. All shitty illusions."

Randy was sprawled on the couch, watching TV.

Some newscaster came on talking about a small town in Montana. Human interest stories. Sad story. Happy story. A kid was killed. *Big deal*, Randy thought bitterly. *Kids get killed every day.*

Then he was there, big as life, talking to the reporters about a trucker who had been lost in a blizzard. "Hey, Teddy, that's my dad," Randy said excitedly. "On TV. That's my dad. Geez, he's still got that shit kickin' grin." Randy listened intently to the rest of the newscast.

When it was all over he went into his bedroom and threw a few jeans and shirts into a backpack. He put on his coat and went back into the living room. Randy touched Teddy on the shoulder as he was leaving. "Later, man," he said softly.

Teddy nodded. "Nothing's real, buddy. Nothing."

Randy went outside and put up his thumb. Clean cut college kid, clean cut college town. He'd get a ride. Once he got to the truck stop out by the interstate it'd be a piece of cake. Somebody there would remember his Dad, give him a ride, Texas bound.

Nothing real? Maybe, maybe not. But he remembered things.

A man with a cocky grin.

An El Paso sunset. A man, a boy, standing beside a truck. The man's eyes looking out over the desert. The boy's eyes looking at the man.

The snow and the ice and the grease and the so damn tired you can't hold your head up and the way his dad would laugh, making it all a game.

Trucking...the playing of the game.

Real things? Maybe, maybe not. It was time to find out. Time to go home.

CHAPTER EIGHT

The young sergeant came and looked in on Jeremy. That woman's words were still ringing in his ears, the red mark her hand had made on his left cheek was still visible.

Damn bitch. Damn old fool doesn't look like he's going to die.

For a minute, driving back to the station, he had wanted to take a side road, wanted to pull over, pull the crazy old fool out of the squad car, kick the living shit out of him.

He hadn't. He was a good cop.

"What'd you think, Sarge? Won't eat a thing."

They moved off down the hall.

"Gonna question him tonight?"

"No, think we'll wait till tomorrow, give him a chance to relax, get use to being here." He was a good cop.

"Think he did it? Seems crazy enough. Been crazy all his life I hear...crazy old retard. Won't even talk. Think he went really crazy, really did that, with the knife?"

The young sergeant shrugged. "Found his prints all over the murder weapon. Only prints on the knife. Don't know," he said. "For a jury to decide, not me." He was a good cop.

They brought him some food but he couldn't eat.
They brought him some water but he couldn't drink.

He stood quietly in a corner, trembling.

Jeremy waited until they were all gone, waited until the only sound was that of tired, caged men breathing deep in their sleep.

He left his corner then and lay down on the cold, dark floor. He lay there for a long time, lay there all through the night, lay there until it was time to go home, to make his circle.

Pre-dawn. The quiet time. Jeremy's time.

Jeremy got up off of the cold dark floor. He was young again. He was the FOX. He lifted his knees proudly, walked quietly out of his cage, quietly through the sleeping town. It was time to go home. Time to make a circle. His circle. Jeremy's circle. Down Canyon Road. Around Ghost Town. Up Blackjack Road to the path that would lead him back to his cabin. His cabin. His circle. Just the right size.

Round.

Complete.

EPILOGUE

Ghost Town is far away from us now. We do not run the Montana hills much anymore and if I am tired, as I often am, I am safe.

Jennifer is not here in the Texas sun. She is at peace, resting peacefully next to my son, near Joe, Jeremy. The inscription on her tombstone is a simple one: JENNIFER DAVIS. BELOVED NEICE OF KATHLEEN O'CONNOR. He shall never have her back. But sometimes, I imagine him still, scalpel in hand, black bag full of strange potions, white hair wild above his distinguished collar, searching endlessly, calling for her, "Jennifer! Little Jennifer?"

Her fame as an artist continues to grow. Many of her paintings have been sold, the funds going to establish the Jennifer Davis Foundation, a foundation dedicated to providing assistance to the victims of childhood sexual abuse.

She belongs to the world and we are far away.

It is better so.

I do not want to live in the past.

Preacher Man is in prison now. The last time the damsel cried someone heard, someone saved her. I had thought that I would hate him, but I do not. Whenever I think of him I feel a terrible sadness. He too was a victim, of other times, other abuses.

I must leave them in peace, as they must leave me, someday, surely in peace.

We are here. We have this day and it is good.

His son came back to him and in his coming brought him renewed gaiety and youth. The boy is much like the man. It has been easy for me to love him. He drives for his dad now and our paths crisscross on a weekly, sometimes daily, basis. There is much laughter during those times.

Brad and Sandy live in a small town near Laredo, Texas. Rob wants Brad to come and work for him as he is buying more new trucks. He is having fun on the road again. Brad just grins and says he's kind of laidback and lazy and not at all sure he wants to work for a hotshot like Rob.

My parents sold Ghost Town the summer after I left. They live in California now, in other hills, soft, warm, green hills. We see them often.

He will come to me soon, come to this table in this crowded truck stop. He will be sweaty, with a smudge of grease or two on his shirt, having been unable to just watch while the mechanics worked on his truck. He will tip his hat back, grin. "You all ready to go?" he will ask.

I will smile, put away my scribbling, my memories.

We climb back in the truck. It is my turn to drive, to stay awake. He settles himself in the bunk, admonishing me to be careful. I turn the key and push the start button. The big rig hums happily. I check my gauges and gently ease into first, releasing the air brakes.

"Rumm, rumm, psst psst," says the big truck.

"Rumm, rumm, pssst, psst, yourself," I say, talking back to it.

It is a warm, starry night. The interstate is all but deserted and I feel a heady sense of freedom as I hit a high cruising speed. The roads are dry, the moon is waxing, and I am headed for the high country.

This is the stuff our lives are made of.

Thank you for reading!

Dear Reader,

I hope you enjoyed reading Ghost Town Truck Stop. I had the idea for this novel thirty years ago and I'm thrilled to share this story and these characters with everyone.

I love to hear from readers, so please share your thoughts about this book with me. You can write to me at barbpaulding@gmail.com.

Finally, I'd like to ask you for a favor. If you're willing, I'd love a review of Ghost Town Truck Stop. I would enjoy getting your feedback. Reviews can be tough to come by. You, as the reader and reviewer, can make or break a book. So, if you have the time, I'd appreciate a review on Amazon.

Thank you so much for reading Ghost Town Truck Stop and for spending time with Katie, Rob, Jennifer, Jeremy and everyone else who was stranded at the Ghost Town Truck Stop.

With heartfelt thanks,

Barbara Paulding

ABOUT THE AUTHOR

Barbara Paulding lives with her husband, Kirk Moody, on a small acreage in southern Iowa. When Barbara was fifty years old, she "ran away from home" and went to truck driving school. She and Kirk drove semis together for two years before she returned to her previous life as a college instructor.

www.ingramcontent.com/pod-product-compliance
Lightning Source LLC
Chambersburg PA
CBHW071302130626
46556CB00003B/1430